DEATH
WARMED
OVER

...

Previous novels by Lee Martin

Murder at the Blue Owl
A Conspiracy of Strangers
Too Sane a Murder

DEATH WARMED OVER

. . .

88-15470

▪ *Lee Martin* ▪

St. Martin's Press
New York

Design by Holly Block

Library of Congress Cataloging-in-Publication Data

Martin, Lee.
    Death warmed over.

    I. Title.
PS3563.A7249D43   1988   813'.54   88-11544
ISBN 0-312-02221-2

First Edition

10 9 8 7 6 5 4 3 2 1

In Memoriam
Barbara Elizabeth Linington
friend and mentor

This novel is fiction. All the people, and most of the places, are entirely made-up. In particular I wish to emphasize that the fictional city of Fort Worth and all its civic employees, and the fictional Postal Inspection Service and all its inspectors, are in no way intended to represent any real people working for the city of Fort Worth or the Postal Inspection Service.

In reality I have never met a postal inspector that I didn't like on sight and appreciate more the more I got to know him.

DEATH
WARMED
OVER

...

1

FROM THE AIR, if you're flying low, the way you can in a small private plane, Fort Worth looks kind of like a patchwork quilt, with blocks of trees and blocks of grassland and blocks of houses and blocks of businesses—and surprisingly, many, many blocks of water. More of the houses than you'd expect have swimming pools; there are streams everywhere; and in the rural areas—of which there are many, even inside the city limits—every little farm has its pond, or more often two or three ponds. Looking down, admiring the blue and green and turquoise of the water belying the brown and tan of the foliage, I wasn't really seeing anything else.

Until my husband Harry said, "Hullo! There's something burning down there."

"Down there where?" I had been simply enjoying one of my rare afternoons off, but my mood abruptly changed. Of course fires aren't my job—I'm a police officer, not a fire fighter—but so often it seems that any kind of anomaly ultimately becomes my job.

"There," Harry repeated unhelpfully, and turned the plane in a tight circle. "Can you see it now?"

"Yeah . . . hold this course." I fumbled for the binoculars Harry always has in the plane, and focused them on the spot. "Oh, lord!"

"What is it? Can you tell yet?"

"Yeah. Get down closer."

In a helicopter—the kind Harry test-pilots during his working hours—we could have set ourselves right down beside it. In this plane we could probably get down safely if we had to, but with the low branches, the thin, almost invisible power and telephone lines, what we probably couldn't do was get back up. But Harry flew as close as he could to the thin column of black smoke; we were almost skimming the tops of the tallest trees.

The smoke was rising from a car. Not a late model car. Dark green. That was all I could tell at first. But then I wasn't paying that much attention to the blazing automobile. I was looking at the pickup truck parked across the road from it. The pickup truck with the sign in the window: U.S. MAIL.

The driver's door on the truck was open. But the driver wasn't out fighting the fire. He was slumped backward, feet out the open door, body sprawled against the console that separated the front bucket seats. And even from the air, with Harry's good binoculars, I could see the red stain that was seeping slowly out to cover his once-white shirt.

"Land," I told Harry, and reached for the radio's hand mike.

"Where?" Harry demanded reasonably.

"I don't care. The closest place you can."

We put it together, later, from what the killer told us, from what the crime scene told us, from what nobody told us but it couldn't have happened any other way, and now, sometimes, in my dreams I see it happening again and again and again, and I seem to be tuning in on the killer's own thoughts the way none of us could that first day, those first weeks.

He hadn't realized, to start with, that a car would be this hard to burn. In the movies it seems the least little thing turns one into a fireball. But he'd found out that motor oil didn't seem to want to ignite. Neither did brake fluid, or ignition fluid. The upholstery wouldn't burn at all. And even that first little puddle of gasoline had flickered dispiritedly for only about two minutes before dying out.

It had been so good a plan, if he could just make it work.

His and Kelly's were just alike—identical forest green 1957 Chevrolet Bel Aires—and of course 1957 was before the vehicle identification number system began. Motor numbers they used then, and the result was that if you changed the motor, then the registration no longer matched the car. Everybody knew that and so nobody checked, just so long as the model and the year matched.

So the first problem was the license plates, and that was simple. He'd taken his own off and put Kelly's on his car. That way, when we found it burned on the side of the road, we'd think it was Kelly's instead of his— easy—and the only harm that could possibly do him was, it might lead us to find Kelly a little sooner. But that wasn't important, because sooner or later we'd find Kelly anyway. Kelly and the other one. By odor, if nothing else.

But by then the car—with that huge, incriminating bloodstain on the back seat, and those other marks inside that so clearly identified it as his—would be no more than a burned-out hulk that nobody would ever be able to trace.

Because the car was on its third engine. Its second was going out when he bought it, and he'd picked up a replacement from a junkyard in Tyler. Paid cash for it, and they'd never even asked his name. With no VIN or inspection sticker, with a motor number that could lead only to a canceled registration, there was no way anyone would ever know it was really his.

That left Kelly's car. It still had the original motor in it, with the original motor number. It could be traced, if there was ever any reason for anybody to take the trouble. But he'd abandon it, with the inspection sticker peeled off and no license plates. If anybody ever did think to look for the motor number and start checking, well, then they'd just have a little bit of a mystery to play with.

Because what they'd have then would be two identical forest green 1957 Chevrolet Bel Aires, one burned and the other abandoned intact, and both of them apparently the same car. It would be confusing, and of course they would try to figure out the discrepancy.

But there was no way anybody would ever trace either one back to him. So nobody could possibly figure out the rest of it.

That was what he hoped. That was what he had planned.

He just hadn't figured on a car being so damned hard to burn.

There it sat, gleaming in the noonday sun, the wax on its smooth paint immaculate, its polished chrome reflecting the late fall colors of the buckeye and the sumac bushes, the never-ending green of the mesquite. That had to be one of the best-looking cars ever made; too bad he had to destroy it. But he did have to. Even Kelly would have realized that now.

He opened the right front door and sniffed as his eyes again fixed on the row of char marks on the seat. None of those ideas had worked. But this one would. He was certain of it. He'd soaked the seats in gasoline and then closed the door, to let the gasoline evaporate into fumes, and now the smell was chokingly strong.

Surely it would catch now.

He stepped back a few paces and hefted the handful of mothballs wrapped in the gasoline-soaked rag. Not very heavy. But heavy enough to throw in this windless late fall day. And nothing like a Molotov cocktail, a bottle that might hold his fingerprints or even the marks of his gloves. He was smarter than that. He touched the cigarette lighter gingerly to the corner of the rag and then let it leave his gloved hand in one smooth practiced motion.

There was a loudly satisfying whoomph and flames shot out every window. It had worked.

He turned to walk back toward Kelly's car, which he'd parked safely on the other side of the tarred road.

And then he saw the mail truck.

We didn't know, as we walked around the burning car, about him, about Kelly and the other one, about the second dark green 1957 Chevrolet Bel Aire.

When it started, though, we didn't know any of it . . . when it started. When did it start? You could trace this one just about as far back as you wanted to. But when he and Kelly drove out on the morning that was to end in Kelly's death, I was with Deborah Mossberg, nursing a headache and wishing to goodness I could be anywhere else but here, working a case that quite obviously was going to turn out not to be a case at all.

"Well, I couldn't have stayed with him any longer," she was telling me, in what she must have assumed was a very reasonable tone of voice. "I mean, look, he was expecting me to support him." She lit a cigarette with shaky hands, replaced the Bic lighter with its fake cloisonné jacket on the cluttered end table, took a large swallow of vodka and orange juice, and regarded me expectantly.

"Uh-huh," I said. "Where are you employed?" She'd dodged that question three times already, and I was beginning to actually want to know why.

"What does that matter?" With a sigh of smoke, Deborah cradled the glowing cigarette between two long, thin, pale, expensively manicured fingertips.

I am pregnant. I cannot handle smoke right now. But I managed not to cough or gag as she went on, "Well, all right. I'm a cocktail waitress. At the Rig."

"The Rig?" I'd never heard of a place with a name like that.

"Yeah. It's like a club, sort of. It gets lots of oil men and they tip real good, only right now—" She shrugged and took another swallow. "Well, I'm not making as much as usual, what with the slowdown in the oil market and all that. And then him expecting to sponge off me like that—and then on top of everything else he had the nerve to say, let's move to Dallas! Just like that, let's move to Dallas. I mean, really!"

"Uh-huh," I said again, drawing a pearl in the oyster shell I'd drawn on my clipboard. This had been dispatched as a kidnapping. It was sounding less and less like one. "Why did he want to move to Dallas?"

"Well, he thought maybe he could find a job there. Look, he could of found a job here if he'd really wanted to. I mean, I did."

I managed not to point out that Rick Mossberg presumably did not possess his former wife's more obvious qualifications. "This oil slump has hurt a lot of people," I commented, hoping that sounded nonjudgmental. I didn't feel nonjudgmental. I didn't like Deborah Mossberg and I especially didn't like the fact that her first name was so much like mine. But police officers can't refuse cases because they don't like the complainant. I went on listening.

"Yeah, but most of them were around Houston, Lubbock," Deborah pouted. "Not here. Not in Fort Worth. And I was driving all the way to Arlington to work. He could of done a little driving too."

From where we were sitting, Arlington was twenty miles away. She'd already told me that the oil company he'd worked for had been drilling all over West Texas; that said Rick Mossberg had done a lot of driving until drilling shut down. But the impact of the oil slump on Texas industry has been incredible. Places that have been booming since the thirties are almost ghost towns; even highly diversified major cities like Dallas, Houston, San Antonio, are feeling the pinch, not just in the oil industry itself but in all the other businesses that serve the oil industry—equipment, chemicals, steel plants that make the pipelines. A lot of men are out of work. Some of them are old; some of them may never have jobs again.

Rick Mossberg was young. But with unemployment so widespread, he wasn't going to find work overnight.

Of course Deborah Mossberg did have a little justice on her side. I could see that it would make more sense to find the job in Dallas or wherever first, and then move.

"All right, you couldn't live with him. So what did you do?" I asked her. Sooner or later we'd get to the missing child. But it had become quite obvious that we'd have to do it Deborah's way; every question I'd asked about the child had been instantly fielded.

"Well, of course, I got a divorce."

"Of course. And then?"

"And the court awarded me child support. Five hundred a month. And the crumb won't pay it."

"If he doesn't have a job—"

"He could of got a job!"

"Okay," I said. "And so?"

"And so of course I said if he wouldn't pay child support then he couldn't have visitation. Don't you think that's fair?"

I decided not to answer that. She wouldn't have liked my answer. "All right, so you wouldn't let him have visitation. And then?"

"Well, and of course I never do see Candy in the evening, because I leave for work about the time she gets out of school, and of course she gets her own breakfast, because I don't get home until so late I just can't get up in the morning. But an hour ago her teacher called to ask me if she was still sick, because they were having some kind of picnic and Candy wasn't there."

"How long has she been sick?"

"Look, I didn't even know she was sick!" Deborah said emphatically. "I mean, if I'd known, of course I'd of stayed home with her. I guess I know my duty. But I know she had breakfast yesterday; I know because she left a mess all over the table, cereal and all, and she left the milk out again. Seems like that girl can't ever remember to put the milk away. And what that stuff costs—" She rolled her eyes and poured another generous slug of vodka into the now very diluted orange juice. "'Course this stuff costs too."

"Uh-huh," I said, because she had paused, evidently expecting an answer.

That must have been answer enough, because she went on. "And then the teacher told me yes, she got sick at school yesterday afternoon, and when they couldn't reach me—I guess I was between home and work, because I left for work early—they called her daddy. And he went up there to get her."

"What time of day was that?"

"About one-thirty, the teacher said. And what I want to know is, what's he still doing with her? He knows—"

"Have you called him?"

"He hasn't got a phone."

"Then how did the school reach him?"

"Well, he's been hanging around this crummy old service station, I mean they pay him a little bit so he calls it working, and they called him there. But he hasn't been there today. I mean I called there and they said they weren't expecting him."

If she says "well" or "I mean" once more I'll scream, I thought. "Have you been to his place?"

"Uh-uh." She flicked ashes into a magenta ashtray. "No, why would I go over there?"

"To see if Candy's there."

Her eyes widened. "Oh, but he's not supposed to have Candy, so if he took her that's kidnapping, isn't it?"

My headache was definitely getting worse. The doctor has forbidden me aspirin, Nuprin, or anything along those lines for the duration. Tylenol maybe? But first I had to answer Deborah Mossberg.

"No, that's not kidnapping. Is there a court order that says he's not supposed to have her?"

"Well, no, but—"

"Is there a court order requiring visitation?"

"Well, yes, but—"

"Do you suspect he might have left town with her?"

"They might of went camping," she said uncertainly.

"Mrs. Mossberg, have you any reason whatever to think that your husband—"

"Ex—"

"Ex-husband," I corrected, "might not intend to return your daughter when the weekend is over?"

Again her eyes widened. Had she been told that expression was cute? Had she been told that was the right way to look at a cop? If so, whoever had told her had not realized that she might get a female cop. But her voice sounded genuinely shocked. "You mean keeping her, not sending her home? Oh, no, Rick wouldn't do anything like that!"

I stood up and closed the cover on my clipboard. "Then you're wasting the police department's time, Mrs. Mossberg, because there's no violation of the law here. I'd suggest, if you're concerned about your daughter, that you go over to your ex-husband's house and see if she's there."

"But—but what if she's not? I mean, the court order just says alternate weekends, not where-all he can take her, and they used to like to go camping."

"Then I'll tell you what, Mrs. Mossberg, since this is Saturday, you call us Monday if she's not back by then, okay?"

I headed for the front door, trying to ignore the querulous voice repeating, "Well, but what if—"

In the car, I massaged my temples wearily, wondering what overexcited idiot of a patrolman had decided this noncase required a detective. From the major case squad, no less.

Of course, if it had been a real kidnapping it would have required somebody from the major case squad. But a few minutes of adroit questioning would have made it clear it wasn't a real kidnapping at all. And I had a hunch she would respond to a male officer a lot better than she did to me.

For the first time I looked farther down the initial complaint, past the name of the complainant, to read the officer's name.

D. Shea.

I might have known.

Danny Shea is a moron, and what I can't figure out about him is how in the world he managed to get on the police department at all, much less survive his six-month review.

Well, Deborah Mossberg would soon be getting another visit from Danny Shea or some other patrol officer, in company with a juvenile officer and a child welfare officer. Because I'd made up my mind that although I was going to unfound this report, I was going to make another one.

Because Candy was six years old. And Candy was left alone seven nights a week, because the two nights a week Deborah wasn't working she was on dates. Candy saw her mother—sometimes—on weekends.

Though Deborah—according to Deborah, at any rate—was very careful to see to it that Candy had clean clothes, had milk, had spending money. (How much spending money does a six-year-old need?) And of course, Deborah assured me righteously, Mrs. Greer was right next door if there was any kind of emergency.

Maybe Rick was as lazy and unambitious as Deborah said he was, or maybe he was a decent man caught in an economic problem he couldn't control. I would decide that later, if I ever had to. But most likely I would never have to think about it again, because most likely Candy would be duly delivered back home—such as it was—sometime Sunday night.

A home from which she should, with any luck at all, be removed sometime Monday to be placed in a decent foster home.

I have friends who are single parents. In a way I was one, before Harry retired from the Marines; while he was overseas, I was at home in Fort Worth working a job that was a lot more demanding, and a lot less well-paying, than the job of a cocktail waitress. My children were never left alone, not at that age, not until they were old enough to have a reasonable amount of good sense.

No child should be left alone like that.

Not at the age of six.

Nearly noon. I wondered how long it would have taken Deborah to realize her daughter was missing if the teacher hadn't called, or whether she would even have noticed that Candy climbed out of Rick's pickup truck instead of the Baptist Church bus when she got home on Sunday evening.

Nearly noon.

At noon I was off. At noon I could go home.

So I drove to our nice, new, already overcrowded police station, parked my police car, went in, and told Captain Millner that this report was unfounded and I was going home.

And I went home, and Harry was home too, and he said, "Let's go flying, before Hal gets home from that Scout shindig."

So we did.

And now, at one o'clock, I was looking at the still-burning hull of an old green Chevrolet, and at a mail truck with a dead mail carrier in the front seat.

Harry, meanwhile, was looking at his plane, which he'd set down on a narrow farm-to-market road, and wondering how he was going to get it back into the air. He wasn't saying much of anything to me.

That was probably just as well. I was pretty sure I didn't want to hear what he was thinking.

But from the air I hadn't been able to tell the man was dead. I could tell he'd been injured, and I could make a reasonable assumption that he'd been shot, but I couldn't know for sure that he was dead. And I'd been hoping that if Harry put the plane down close enough, I could get right to him, in less than the ten or twenty or more minutes it might take to get an ambulance here. I might have been able to do him some kind of good.

I hoped I could help him.

Not just because he was a mail carrier. I knew him. Even from the air I knew him, because I knew that truck. I thought he'd retired.

Correct that. I knew he'd retired.

Roy Bassinger had been a rural mail carrier for fifty years. He had retired only last July, very proud that in fifty years he'd never missed a scheduled day on his route in the northeast corner of Tarrant County, Texas. But even after he'd retired he couldn't stay away. He kept coming back in to help, because he didn't want to see everything all messed up. He told me that a couple of weeks ago when I met him in the post office; he said he'd asked to be called as relief whenever his replacement was sick.

Which, he said, seemed to be kind of often.

Roy Bassinger was seventy-two.

And now Roy Bassinger was dead, shotgunned in the front seat of his own garishly hand-painted red-white-and-blue pickup truck, the truck he'd proudly identified with a hand-lettered U.S. Mail sign in the front window.

A postal inspector I met once called rural mail carrier the best job in the post office. But this time it hadn't been.

A car bumped over the dirt road and stopped, fast, and a door slammed. I turned to see Otto Castillo—a funny name for a postal inspector, a funny name for anybody; he'd told me his father was Cuban and his mother was German—picking his way around the plane. He was parked on the other side of it.

Traffic was being rerouted both ways. Fortunately, there wasn't much traffic to reroute.

All right, I goofed. As Harry might say—if Harry happened to be speaking to me right now—Mama did a dumb-dumb.

But Harry goofed too.

We had not picked a very good place to land a single-engine private plane, and I had a hunch I was going to be hearing about this for quite a while, from quite a few people.

Otto was not, at the moment, concerned about where anybody had parked an airplane. He approached the truck, looked in it, and said, "Damn."

He didn't, for the moment, say anything else. He just stood and looked.

Then he said, "We're going to nail that bastard."

"Sure," I said. For want of anything better to say. I mean, how do you respond to that sort of assertion?

He looked at me, coldly.

There are female postal inspectors now. There have been policewomen in some places (not, of course, Fort Worth) since the turn of the century.

But Otto Castillo is no believer in equal rights, and he was not going to enjoy working with me. He was going to have to work with me anyway. In the Fort Worth Police Department, the first detective on the scene—unless there is a pressing reason otherwise, and Otto Castillo's prejudice would not be considered a pressing reason—gets the case. And in a situation like this, federal and local cooperation was essential.

It wasn't that Otto Castillo didn't like me, you understand. He likes me just fine. He's said so, several times. He just feels I should keep my place. Which, according to him, definitely is not in a police department. Or if I do idiotically insist on being a police officer, I should work something genteel, like juvenile.

Need I mention that Otto has not been around many juveniles lately?

He was still glaring at me. In his anger, he had not yet noticed my attire or my midsection. I wondered how he was going to react when he found out that not only did he have to work with a female, he had to work with a pregnant female.

"Sure," he repeated. "Sure. Sure, you say. That makes a lot of sense. Look, Deb Ralston, this is no quilting bee here. We've got an army of mail carriers. They go on foot, alone, carrying checks, where police go in pairs and armed. If we don't make an example of it any time one of them gets hit, how long—"

"I hear you," I told him.

"So if it costs a million dollars, if it costs four million dollars, if we have to fly a lab team in from Memphis, if we have to fly dogs in, if we have to—"

"I said I hear you," I repeated.

"Fine. You hear me. Now what in the hell do you intend to do about it?"

"There's plenty I'm going to do about it, Otto," I told him. "I've just got a whole head full of ideas about what I'm going to do. Now what are you going to do about it?"

He didn't answer. He glared at me for another moment or two and then stalked back to his car, where I suppose he got on a radio or car phone to discuss what he was going to do.

In most places postal inspectors work alone, but Fort Worth is one of their regional offices, and if he needed to he could get a whole battalion of postal inspectors in. Well, not exactly a battalion, I guess. Ten, maybe, or twelve. But for postal inspectors that's a lot. They tend to be smarter than FBI or Secret Service people, partly, I guess, because they are used to working alone.

Nicer, too, usually. Especially than the FBI.

Of course there are exceptions. There are always exceptions.

I continued to stand and look at the still-smoldering old car. Eventually the fire department would arrive. I'd heard their sirens every now and then as they attempted to maneuver a large fire truck over unpaved back roads to get around Harry's plane (look, I've already admitted I goofed) to reach the fire. Which, by now, had almost burned itself out anyway.

If the trees had caught, we'd have been in big trouble. But fortunately they didn't.

A patrol car was already here, sitting on the other

side of the plane beside Otto's car, with two patrol officers in it.

I found it difficult to believe we were actually inside the city limits of Fort Worth—I'd have been glad to hand this case to the county investigators—but the dispatcher I'd talked with on the patrol car's radio had assured me the case was ours whether we wanted it or not. The city boundaries, he said, do odd things every now and then.

I supposed the patrolmen were guarding the crime scene.

Not that there was likely to be much guarding necessary; nobody ever comes here. There are, maybe, six houses on Four Mile Road; at the end the road turns to the left and becomes a little dirt footpath that trails down to one of the umpteen branches of one of the umpteen creeks that ultimately feed into the Trinity River. It is a very useless little branch—there's a pond in it, but you can't possibly fish or swim there because it's full of gar. The time Harry and Hal tried to fish in it they got a six-foot gar and Hal, too excited to listen to Harry's warning, tried to behead it with an ax and of course the ax broke. A gar, in case you don't know, has jaws like an alligator's, containing about a million razor-sharp teeth. I've seen one bite an oar in two. A good, new oar. On top of that gars are armor-plated. They have, I'm told, survived in the very same form they're in now since before the age of the dinosaurs. I can imagine why. I'm certainly not going to dispute anything with a gar. I suspect that nothing short of a full-grown *Tyrannosaurus rex* would try that.

Anyhow, although I'd lived in Fort Worth all my life I hadn't even known there was a road to the left off Four Mile Road. A driveway, that was all I knew about—the kind of driveway that is actually sort of a private road leading to a farm. The whole left side of Four Mile Road borders the farm.

But the driveway was tarred and the city maps now called it Kelly Road, although it went exactly nowhere except to the old Joe Kelly farm, which to the best of my knowledge had been abandoned at least fifteen years ago. I'd been expecting it would be sold for back taxes, and some housing development would mushroom up where the Kelly cows used to graze.

The old farmhouse most likely was still there, although it was surely unoccupiable after all these years, and nobody, yet, had put anything else there.

But for some reason the mail truck had turned onto Kelly Road, and there it might have sat for a month, with Bassinger dead in the front seat, if Harry and I hadn't seen the smoke and come to investigate.

Come to think of it, since we had at least discovered the crime quickly, there was a chance I would be forgiven for having caused Harry to land his plane on Kelly Road. Of course it would have been better if he'd landed on the Kelly farm side of the burning car, instead of on the Four Mile Road side of it.

But I couldn't do anything about that now.

The fire truck finally arrived, swooping in with great panache and loud sirens and horns, all trying to mask the fact that it was traveling at a majestic fifteen miles per hour. I waved at the driver to stop and he ignored my signal, turtling right past me to park directly on top of the place where the suspect—whoever the suspect was—might have left tire tracks.

I was, of course, assuming that the suspect was driving something. I hadn't actually seen any tire tracks, and he might just as well have been walking. Probably he had been, if that was his burned-out car, as it very likely was. Oh well—on this sandy stretch of road, probably the tracks wouldn't have been usable anyway, even if the fire truck hadn't parked on top of them.

The fire fighters set about with great vigor, spraying water and some sort of chemicals on the now barely smoking car, and I stood and watched them. At least watching them was a good way to keep from looking at Bassinger's body.

I guessed Bassinger had turned onto the road—for what reason I couldn't imagine—and caught somebody in the act of arson. And the arsonist, panicky, had killed him to prevent Bassinger from telling what he saw.

By now we should know who the car belonged to, only it was Saturday and the county files were unavailable and TCIC—the Texas crime computer that links police, state, and local offices—was down. Sooner or later we'd find out; it was a very simple crime.

And so totally futile.

The old man, his sparse white hair not fully covering his pink scalp, was sprawled in the cab of the truck, his body slumped to the right and leaning back. The driver's door still hung open, just as it had when I first saw it from the air, so that we could easily see the extent of the damage. It was a chest wound, a big one; we wouldn't know for sure until the medical examiner was through, but for now I was guessing some sort of shotgun. The wound was too big for any rifle or handgun I could think of. But on the other hand, it hadn't been made by the biggest shotgun around, either, not unless it had been fired at contact range.

Which it hadn't been, or there'd have been powder blackening on the white shirt visible even through the blood.

So, a small shotgun. Maybe a .410, maybe a snake gun. Or maybe, just maybe, a load of snake shot in a .38 or a .357.

A stupid kill, of a harmless victim, to cover up a common crime. Just arson. And even if it was arson for profit, what kind of insurance can you get on a car that old? $200? $300? Hardly enough to be worth paying the premiums.

So why bother to torch it?

That was what I thought then.

On some matters I am remarkably ill-informed.

· 2 ·

"I'm sorry," I told Harry.

"You damn well ought to be." He was still staring at his airplane. "Now how in the hell am I going to get this thing up from here?"

The answer was quite obvious, and he knew it as well as I did. He was going to have to get a police escort to clear the road as he taxied all the way back to Four Mile Road and onto a long stretch with no power lines, so that he could take off.

He was going to have to do it without me. And even so he was going to have to wait a while. Between the plane's landing kicking up dust, and the fire truck's arrival kicking up more dust, there was precious little potential evidence likely to be left on the ground. But that little we wanted to be able to preserve. Otto Castillo, muttering imprecations in English, Spanish, German, and something else I think might have been Aztec, had departed temporarily, after threatening both me and the patrolmen guarding the scene with mayhem if unauthorized persons approached the mail truck.

Unauthorized persons, according to Castillo, included Harry. So not only couldn't he leave, he also couldn't get close enough to see what was going on. In fact, at the moment he couldn't even get back to the plane. He had walked through the crime scene area, on an absolutely featureless tarred road, to the patrol car, and Castillo had ordered him to stay there. Meanwhile, of course, assorted other people including Captain Millner, deputy medical examiner Andrew Habib, his investigator Gil Sanchez, and our own crime scene tech Irene Loukas were strolling past him. Habib was whistling merrily as is his wont when approaching homicides; later he'd start humming under his breath. Not humming like singing without words. Making noises like "hmm" and "uh-huh" and "mm-huh" like a dentist with his head in some victim's mouth.

I think Habib is sort of strange. But he's undeniably a good medical examiner.

Sanchez, almost to the mail truck, turned. "Hey, Deb," he yelled, "you want to come tell us just what you've got going on here?"

"I'm sorry," I told Harry again.

He didn't answer; at least he didn't answer me. He said something under his breath to Bill Livingston, who was still sitting at the wheel of the patrol car (that's how much guarding the crime scene needed) and I heard Bill laugh as I trudged back down the tarred road.

Habib paused directly in front of me, staring at the burnt green car, and whistled. "Son of a bitch," he said.

"Huh?" I said.

"What vandal—" Habib's voice was shaking with rage as he gently touched one blackened green tail fin.

"Huh?" I repeated. I looked at the car too. It still looked to me like an old—a very old—green car.

"Deb, that's a fifty-seven Chevrolet!"

"Okay," I said. "So what? That makes it about thirty-odd years old, right?"

He muttered something that sounded like a rather garbled advertising jingle. "Task force fifty-seven Chevrolets, test on the Alcan Run."

"Huh?" I said for the third time, this time I think pardonably. "Andy, what kind of bee have you got in your bonnet now?"

He looked at me. "You really don't know?"

"No. I really don't know. All I see is an old dead car. You obviously see something I don't."

"Oh hell. Yeah. Obviously I see something you don't." He assumed his professorial lecture mode. "Well, now, let's see, about fifty-five, fifty-six, somewhere in there, cars started having tail fins, and later on, by fifty-nine, sixty, the tail fins had grown into real monstrosities. But the fifty-seven Chevrolet, Deb, was the very best use of the tail fins. It was—is—a good-looking car. A classic. People collect them. It's just not a car somebody would burn for the insurance money or because he wanted to be rid of a junker, that's all."

"Unless he didn't know—"

"He wouldn't not know. If you're driving a fifty-seven Chevrolet—or if you have one up on blocks behind your house, for that matter—people will be stopping, asking to buy it."

"But if—"

"Anyway," Habib added firmly, "somebody's been

taking care of this one. Look, see how smooth it is here, where the fire never got to the wax job?"

I looked. He was right. Somebody had been taking care of this car.

"Thing is," he added, "you could sell this baby any day of the week for a hell of a lot more than you could insure it for. And you damn sure wouldn't burn it as rubbish, because it's not rubbish. You could sell the shell of one for—"

"Okay," I interrupted. I had no doubt that he was right. I can't think of a time when I've ever caught Andrew Habib, with all his multitudinous hobbies, not being right. But if it wasn't burned for the insurance, and it wasn't burned as rubbish—"That car didn't catch on fire by itself. Somebody set it on purpose. I'm sure of that, because the interior's gutted and the engine area hardly even caught. And Andy, it is some more kind of hard to burn the interior of a car."

"Is it?" Habib sounded dubious. Then he shrugged. "I guess you know."

"I know. I've been to some arson schools. I've worked some arson cases."

Habib was still looking at the car. "Then he was a world-class son of a bitch."

"Because he burned a fifty-seven Chevrolet. Never mind that he also murdered an old man." My voice must have sounded rather caustic.

"Well, that too," Habib said, and reluctantly turned his attention to the corpse.

He could do that now; all the necessary photographs of the body and the truck had been taken, and the necessary but futile efforts to lift prints from the truck—necessary because they were a part of working a crime scene, futile because there was no earthly reason why

the killer ever had to approach the truck to start with—
had been made.

Habib poked for a while and hmmed for a while, until
I reminded him he had to pronounce the victim dead.
He turned, looking startled. "Huh? Oh, well, yes, of
course he's dead."

"Thank you, doctor, for that legal formality." I made a
note on a piece of scratch paper scrounged from the
floorboard of the airplane. I do not carry my notebook
with me on personal flights; in fact, I very improperly
was not even armed at the moment. "Victim pro-
nounced dead by Dr. Andrew Habib on the scene at—"
I consulted my watch—"two-oh-two P.M."

I continued to watch, uneasily, as Habib continued to
poke and hmm. I don't too much like to work cases in
which I know the victim, because it's too hard for me to
think of it as just a case, the victim as just a victim, a
nameless part of the background scenery necessary to
make up part of the crime scene. I remembered the
time two police officers I knew well had been shot
while serving a search warrant. They'd both survived,
luckily, but we hadn't known until days later that they
were going to. I was on the crime scene crew then.

I was on the crime scene crew, and I was at the Elks
Lodge, playing bingo and drinking beer, and somebody—a sergeant—came and got me out of the bingo
hall and we left together, but after a while we decided
to wait and work the scene when it was daylight. So the
patrolman delivered me back to the lodge where Harry
was patiently waiting for me, and I rejoined him in the
bar because bingo was over, and I changed my drink
from beer to old-fashioneds. They're kind of strong, but
that night it was like drinking water.

We finally went home, and early the next morning I

got up and went to the scene. The victims were intelligence officers, and so intelligence was serving the search warrant while ident worked the crime scene.

We all survived—we all kept going—by never saying their names. Never saying their ranks. Always saying the victims. The victims. If they were only the victims, not Steve and Dale, we could go on working.

And so we did, until late that afternoon, when one of the intelligence officers, walking in the front yard and carefully not seeing the blood-soaked gauze squares and the other paraphernalia the ambulance crew had left behind, caught a glimpse out of the corner of his eye of something gold glinting on the ground. He knelt. "What is this?" he asked.

And another intelligence officer, standing right behind him, stepped around him and knelt too. "It's Steve's Saint Christopher," she said, and stood holding the broken chain and the little gold medallion in her hand.

And we all, the five police officers left at the scene, stood and stared at the broken chain with the little gold medallion on it. Steve's Saint Christopher, that we were used to seeing around Steve's neck, with the medallion resting just at the V of his undershirt. It wasn't "the victims" any longer. It was Steve and Dale and we loved them and we didn't know if they were going to live or die.

At last Gina said, almost under her breath, "I'll take it to him."

It was part of the crime scene. I should have laid it back in the grass. I should have photographed it, and put it in a little plastic sack, and sealed it away until after the trial.

But I couldn't. "Yes," I said, "yes, you do that. You take it to him."

We'd ordered bulletproof vests for people likely to be in tough situations. When we got back into the office, with all our photographs and all our evidence and Steve's Saint Christopher medal, the man from UPS was there delivering the vests. We opened the boxes and their sergeant got one of the vests out and held it in his hands for a long time, and looked at it. He didn't say that the shipment was three weeks late. He didn't say that Steve and Dale should have been wearing those vests the night before. He didn't say anything. He just held the vest in his hands and looked at it for a long time, and then he put it back in the box and walked away, not quite steadily, toward the men's restroom.

I didn't cry. Not then. I just wrote my report and went home and started drinking again, and finally, a long time later, while Johnny Carson was being funny on television, I drew my knees up in my chair and sat with my face against my knees and sobbed. I don't know how long I cried.

Gina told me later she went home and cried for two hours.

Their sergeant told me later he went home and got drunk and cried.

Their lieutenant told me he went out to the target range and K-fived the hell out of a lot of targets.

My partner—a tough ex-boxer-turned-cop (that was after Clint Barrington went over to the sheriff's office)—told me he went home and got as drunk as he could and spent the rest of the night until 5:00 A.M. with his head in the toilet alternating between vomiting and crying. I could believe it. Even before he insisted on showing me the toilet-rim-shaped bruise on his chest.

I wasn't going to get drunk and cry about this. I hadn't known the old man that well; besides that, my doctor has been very stern about something called fetal alcohol syndrome, and I am not allowed to get closer than five feet to anything with drinkable alcohol in it right now. I might decide to cry, but then again I might not. Whether I did or not, it would be at home on my own time. I neither cry nor vomit at crime scenes.

So I just stood and looked at the old man leaning back in the blood-spattered interior of the pickup truck. Pale blue eyes, red-rimmed, stared vacantly through gold-framed bifocals that hung askew on the cherubic pink face; the mouth gaped to disclose the too-perfect pearliness of an old set of dentures. The white shirt of some silky-looking synthetic was pulled open over a white cotton undershirt—crew-necked, not V-necked—and blood had splattered over the old man's expensive gold pocketwatch.

Irene Loukas and Bob Castle were going over the ground now, looking for anything that could either lead us to the killer or help us to pin the crime to him after we had identified him through other means. I expected it was a futile effort; the hard black tar surface wasn't going to tell anyone anything, and what ground there was had been sprayed with flying dirt and debris from the airplane's propeller and then soaked with water and chemicals from the fire truck.

And the victim hadn't been shot from close range anyway. There was no reason the killer ever had to get off the tar.

Habib turned and threw out an order to move the body. As an afterthought, he added, "The postal inspector is through with it, isn't he?"

"I don't know where the postal inspector went," I replied.

"I'm right here." Otto Castillo was on his way back,

with a semisatisfied look on his face. "Yeah, you can go on and move the body, but don't touch anything else in the truck."

Habib turned slowly, to look again at the truck. "Mister," he said, "that body weighs about two hundred and fifty pounds. You want to get him out without touching anything else in the truck?"

"That's not what I mean," Castillo said impatiently. "I mean the mail, that kind of thing. I've got to take custody of it and see that it gets delivered."

"Delivered?"

"Delivered," Castillo repeated. "That's the law. The mail has to get delivered. Just give me the keys, and when you get through with the body lock up the truck. And leave a patrolman to guard it."

"Mister, that's not my job," Habib said.

"I'll see to it the scene is protected," I told him.

"Good, now if you'll excuse me—" He began to walk on down Kelly Road.

"Where are you going?" I asked sharply.

"None of your business."

"The hell it's none of my business. This is my case too. Where are you going?"

He didn't like it. But I was right and he knew it. "We got a make on the license plates," he disclosed reluctantly. "One Patrick Kelly. Address on Kelly Road."

"But I thought nobody lived—"

"Is this Kelly Road?"

"This is Kelly Road. But—"

"Then I'm going to go and look at Patrick Kelly."

"And I'm coming with you," I said. "Just let me get a radio."

"Why in the world do you want a—"

"One time I got in a shootout and I didn't have a radio with me," I said, not adding that it was only months ago. "I'm never going to do that again."

"You planning to get in a shootout?"

"No. But I wasn't planning to then, either."

Castillo shrugged, and I borrowed Bill Livingston's walkie-talkie. That left him with only the radio in his car, but as he didn't seem to be planning to get out of his car anyway, that should be no handicap.

The doctor told me I ought to do a lot of walking. I was certainly doing it today; it was a good mile from the crime scene to the point where the road dead-ended into an old farm road.

An old farm that was no longer quite as ramshackle as it had been the last time I saw it, which was probably four years ago. Somebody had recently made a little effort to clean it up. The yard had been cut not with a lawn mower but with a tractor, leaving stubble six inches high, and debris had been piled up in one corner of the road—most likely they'd been waiting until after the next rain to burn it, because despite September's heavy rain the woods and fields were still tinder-dry in places. Somebody had begun painting the house a garish yellow, and a tall ladder leaned against the front wall beside a second-story window. There were tire tracks and footprints in the rutted dirt of the driveway.

A black and tan feist stood up at our approach and stretched its front legs, hindquarters ridiculously in the air, and then straightened again, wagging its tail and whining a welcome before walking anxiously to an empty metal pan on the front porch. It wasn't a food pan; there was a spilled sack of dry dog food beside it. I detoured to a water hose, and the dog drank eagerly from the nozzle, not waiting for the dish to fill.

Castillo watched me, his face impassive, and then

when I was beside him again he knocked on the door frame. On the door frame, because the wooden storm door stood open and the old screen door sagged.

This was stupid. One of us should have been at the back door. Should I, or should I not, tell Castillo his business?

Wads of dusty cotton were stuck with hairpins into the black mesh of the screen to scare the flies away, and the wooden molding that held the screen in place hadn't been repainted yet. Its old gray paint was chalky, cracked, falling into powder.

Nobody was going to have to tell Castillo his business.

Nobody was coming out the back door. Nobody would be in that house, now, by choice. I could hear the flies buzzing, and I could smell what they were buzzing about.

Castillo sniffed and turned away, roughly taking me by the arm and turning me too. "What are you doing?" I asked.

"You don't need to go in there," he told me, in a rough attempt at gallantry. "Isn't that medical examiner, what's his name, Philip Habib—"

"Philip Habib is an ambassador," I interrupted. "The medical examiner is Andrew Habib."

"You can get him out here. You know what's in this house." Castillo opened the door.

"No, I don't know what's in this house," I said.

"You and I both know—"

"No, Otto, you're wrong," I said. "I know the condition of what's inside this house. That's all I know. I don't know what's inside the house. And I have to find out. You don't. You're a postal inspector. Your case is down the road. But that's my case in there, and I have to go in. You can go with me if you want to. But you don't have to."

Castillo let go of my arm. I opened the screen door.

A dusty entry hall, dimly lit in the early afternoon, dark with hardwood floors and stair risers partly covered with fraying dusty rose carpeting. Brown-painted banisters flanked the stairs; brown-stained doors were closed on the left and the right of the narrow hall that led straight ahead, passing to the right of the staircase and leading to a third closed brown door. Generations of beetles had left their carapaces along the baseboards, and the floral wallpaper was smudged with spider webs.

"Nobody could have been living here," Castillo said. But he sounded uncertain.

The smell was stronger inside, and the buzzing of flies continued somewhere toward the left and farther back. Except for that, the silence was complete.

Castillo's right hand was now resting on his gun butt. I didn't mind that; in fact, I thought it was a pretty good idea. With his left hand, he caught hold of the first doorknob. He flung the door open and back hard against the wall, sending something crashing to the floor. The crash seemed to echo into silence, and the only other sound was the buzzing, louder yet, of flies. The smell, with the opening of the door, abruptly became stronger.

An ornate Victorian loveseat reupholstered in a beige chintz printed in huge cabbage roses was blackened with mold as if with a fire; overhead a huge stain on the ceiling told of old unmended leaks in the roof. Two Queen Anne chairs, similarly upholstered, flanked a rickety round piecrust table topped with an ornate kerosene lantern bedecked with jet beads and glass prisms that now, in the semidarkness, sent no rainbows flashing. The blackened fireplace was empty of everything but rusted firedogs, more beetle shells, and a little rubbish that might have been swept from the floor.

The crash had been a porcelain vase, knocked off a long wall table by the slam of the door.

Belatedly, I began to wonder if we had the right to be in here at all. The Supreme Court has ruled that we now have to have search warrants to search crime scenes, and of course our rights to enter private property have always been somewhat limited.

But surely, any reasonable person, police officer or not, smelling what we were smelling, would go to investigate. Surely the courts would take that into consideration. "In here," I said, taking the lead again.

An old linoleum floor, vaguely greenish but trodden and scrubbed into a weathered white in most places. A gas stove sitting up on four curved pale green legs, blackened with old grease, the porcelain chipping off the underlying cast iron. A white enameled table and two old metal and yellow Formica chairs. One electric light bulb, hundred watt, dangled from bare wires above a small single sink to light the room.

The light was on, and a horde of flies buzzed over something wrapped in a quilt and lying on the kitchen floor.

I leaned over for a better look.

Maybe this was Patrick Kelly. I didn't know. But even if I had known him I couldn't say now who this was. The shotgun blast had caught him in the lower jaw at least two days ago, and rodents—I guessed rats or opossums—had come in the open back door and chewed on the body, so that the facial skin was utterly gone, exposing not yet decaying muscle attached to clean bone.

Behind me, I could hear Otto Castillo pausing. Like me, he must be staring at the articulated jawbone laid bare by the scavengers.

"I never saw anything like that before," he said.

"Me neither," I agreed, unable to tear my eyes away. "Kind of Vincent Price, isn't it?"

"Uh-uh. Not gruesome enough. It ought to be but it's not. It's almost—it's almost like some sort of biological exhibit demonstrating the facial muscles and bones. Well." I heard a long, indrawn breath. "For sure it's going to take fingerprints to identify that one. Did you get a look at the hands?"

"They're okay." They were. It wasn't hot; the hands had scarcely begun to rot. Bitten fingernails. White hairs sprouting from fingers marked by swollen knuckles—arthritis, maybe? Worn hands, blistered but not callused, not roughed—he hadn't done much heavy manual work until recently; those blisters told of recent unaccustomed labor. Jailhouse tattoos—L-O-V-E along the lower finger joints of the right hand, H-A-T-E on the other. That didn't necessarily prove anything, but it suggested a lot.

One thing it suggested was that it might be fairly easy to get him identified, whether or not he was Patrick Kelly—and suddenly I remembered who Patrick Kelly was.

But—the hands in good condition, the face eaten by rodents but not in bad shape otherwise; what was that saying to me?

Otto, surprisingly, realized before I did. "That smell's from something else. Where?"

And then I knew. Almost before I knew I was going to do it, I stood up, turned, pushed open the ill-fitting door of the walk-in pantry behind me, and involuntarily screamed. Otto turned sharply. "What the hell?"

I don't usually scream on the job. In fact I don't think I ever have done it before. But I was reaching out blindly for comfort. "Oh, no, I had a complaint today of a missing child and I wouldn't even take the report, because—"

"How old a child? Girl or boy?" Otto's voice sounded as shaken as I felt. But he wasn't the one who hadn't taken the report.

"Girl. Six. Six—just a baby really. If this is her—"

"This isn't a six-year-old and she's been dead—how long? Longer than the one in the kitchen, but how long? You've got more experience with this kind of thing than I do. How long? Longer than the one you heard about today that's missing?"

"This one—a week, maybe. Maybe not—or maybe more. It's cool now but I don't know, they might have had the heat on before and that would—accelerate it, depending—" I was calming fast. He was right. This definitely wasn't Candy Mossberg. "You're right. This is a different one. She's maybe nine or ten? But where'd she come from? We haven't had any reports of—"

"A parochial school would be my guess," Otto said. "I mean, judging by the clothes."

Dark green and blue plaid skirt, knife pleated. A plaid vest and blue blazer over a short-sleeved white blouse. No coat. She should have had a coat. The mornings are cold now, and no matter what the weather report says, a blue norther is always a possibility this late in the year. But no coat. No sweater. White knee socks, one black kiltie loafer—the other missing somewhere—and brown hair.

And it was to be hoped she'd had a dental chart, because she might never be legally identified otherwise. There must be hundreds of flies, thousands of maggots; the draining body fluids had collected in puddles on the floor, and drained through cracks in places into the subfloor or onto the ground underneath the house, and ants had tracked up following the smell. The face, for all practical purposes, was gone. The ridged skin of the fingertips, always delicate and fragile on so young a child, was certainly gone.

Nothing to say for sure how she'd died. Just that her hands and feet had been tied when it happened.

· 3 ·

"Look, we try to avoid publicity in a case like this," FBI agent Darren Fletcher said. "And we had no reason whatever to suppose she'd been moved out of the Dallas area. I mean, we were working it as if she had, because it was over twenty-four hours and there was a ransom demand and we had to assume the possibility that—but damn it, there was just no reason—"

"Well, she's sure as hell here," the other FBI man, a youngster named Eddie Cohen I'd met briefly about a year ago, said. "Unless there's another kid missing from Saint Ursula's."

"Don't even think it," Fletcher told him. He turned to Millner, who is technically my boss's boss and head of the criminal investigation division. "Dallas'll be getting with you about it."

Habib, hmming around the larger body, looked up incredulously. "Dallas'll be getting—wait a minute, are you saying the FBI won't be working this?"

I started to answer, but Neal Ryan, a rather bookish-looking man whose only concession to the traditional concept of the Texas Rangers is his pair of hand-tooled leather boots, beat me to it. "It's not a federal crime."

"But I thought kidnapping was always—"

"Uh-uh," Fletcher said. "Not if it's intrastate."

What was Habib arguing about anyway, I wondered. He wasn't working the case. All he was supposed to be doing was finding the cause of death, which, in the case of the mail carrier and Patrick Kelly, was quite obvious. And he hadn't even gotten to the girl's body yet.

"But I thought after so many hours—" he continued to protest.

Fletcher didn't quite sigh, but his expression sighed for him. "After twenty-four hours, if it looks like a real snatch—or we'll ignore the twenty-four-hour rule if there's a ransom demand or if it looks heavy otherwise—then the legal assumption is that it's gone interstate and we enter the case. But if the victim then turns up instate, alive or dead, it's not our case. We'll assist all anybody asks us to, and be glad to do it. But the jurisdiction belongs to the state of Texas, and to the city of Dallas where the snatch took place, and to the city of Fort Worth where the body turned up."

"And that's the way it is and that's the way it's going to be," Captain Millner added. "Deb—"

"I know," I said. "I'm on it, so stay on it."

"That's a right tactful way of putting it," Millner said.

"I'm on it too," Ryan said. He added, "I don't like this kind of case. Murdered kids, I mean, I don't like murdered kids. All right. Sequence. Kelly—if that one over there is Kelly, and it probably is—teamed up with somebody else to pull the kidnapping. So they pulled it, and then they hightailed it back here to hide the kid. So the kid died, or they killed her, or something, but they picked up the ransom anyway. Of course."

"Of course," I echoed, trying to imagine the kind of mind that would value money over the life of a child. I couldn't imagine it. I was glad I couldn't.

"So they went to quarreling," Ryan went on. "So he—whoever he was—shot Kelly. And then went and burned Kelly's car, which makes no sense whatever, and the postman caught him at it and he shot the postman. Agreed?"

"Mail carrier," Castillo said remotely.

"What?" Ryan asked.

"Mail carrier. Not postman any longer. We've got both sexes. Mail carrier."

"Okay," Ryan said. "So now all we've got to do is find out who did it, and where he is right now, and where did he put the two hundred and fifty grand. And none of it's a federal crime. So why," he demanded, "have we got the FBI and the postal inspector?"

"He killed a mail carrier," Castillo said. "You think that's not a federal crime?"

"Of course that is, but that didn't happen here, and—"

"It's tied in. It's got to be."

"Okay. But why the FBI?"

"To assist," Fletcher said delicately.

I understood Ryan's objections. I felt the same way, most of the time. It's this way: If the FBI and the local police do something together, the headlines say "FBI Clears Case." The FBI likes publicity—a lot of it. If the local police and the Secret Service work together, the headlines say "Local Police and Secret Service Clear Case." The Secret Service likes publicity, too, but not as much as the FBI does.

Given a choice, most local police would rather work

with the postal inspectors. Because then the headlines say "Local Police Clear Case." The postal inspectors don't like publicity.

But this time I didn't care who got the headlines. I just wanted the case cleared, the sooner the better.

"I'd be glad to go home," the younger FBI agent— Cohen—offered boisterously, his voice loud in the quiet room. "That stinks in there."

Fletcher turned to stare at him, and he was suddenly quite still. "Sorry," he muttered.

Cohen had seen violent death before. I knew that because I was with him the first time he saw it. He ran out the front door to vomit in the flower bed. He'd come a long way since then—he hadn't vomited at the sight of the child—but still, a child violently dead shakes anybody the first time. And the five-thousandth time. You get used to the adults, but never to the children.

Castillo didn't seem to have heard him at all. "Damn it, I knew Bassinger," he said, "and there's not much more reason for killing him than there was for killing that poor kid in there—what did you say her name was?"

"French. Helen French. Her daddy runs a big Chevrolet agency on Central Expressway in Dallas."

"Only child?" Millner asked. So often it does seem that kidnap victims are only children.

"Fifth of eight," Fletcher answered. "It matter any? I've got five. You don't love 'em any less just because you've got more. Oh hell—somebody call somebody to move the damn bodies." He turned away, but not before I saw tears standing in his brown eyes.

"I don't even know where to start," I said, poking miserably at a single strand of lettuce decorated with a frail splash of salad dressing.

"You can start by eating your supper," Harry said.

Otto Castillo, who had joined us for dinner at Cattleman's, looked from me to Harry and back at me. He didn't say anything, but I knew what he was thinking. I could see the disgusted look on his face, and frankly, at this moment I didn't care. I wasn't supposed to be on duty at all today; I'd gone in during the morning because we had several people in court. I'd taken off at noon to go spend time with my family, and now, at seven-thirty, I was back in the middle of a case and it was perfectly obvious my weekend was shot again. I should be feeling sorry for the old mail carrier, and for the little girl, and for their families, and I was. But I was also feeling sorry for myself—idiotically so.

Harry was still looking pointedly at my empty fork. I put it down beside my plate. "I'm not hungry," I said. "I ate those barbecue sandwiches—"

"Seven hours ago. Almost." Harry sounded annoyed.

"What?" I said.

"Seven hours ago, almost, you had a barbecue sandwich. One. Not several. And I'm not sure you finished it. Eat your supper. The kid's not going to get any less dead for your brooding about it."

I picked up a small bite of salad, chewed it thoroughly, swallowed, and took a sip of ice water. "I'm not hungry."

"Are you coming down with something?" Castillo demanded. Quite incredibly, he still hadn't noticed my attire or my midsection, or else he had noticed and it just hadn't registered.

"No, I'm not coming down with something," I snapped, and ate the rest of my salad as fast as I could while the waitress approached with plates of steak and potatoes.

"Is Patrick Kelly local?" Otto Castillo asked.

"Yeah. What makes you ask?"

"At the scene you said you knew who Patrick Kelly is. Or was. What do you mean? It's not as if this were some little one-horse village; Fort Worth's not as big as Dallas but all the same it's a good-sized city. What do you mean, you know who Patrick Kelly was?"

"It was a big story a long time ago," I told him. "I was in high school when it happened."

"When what happened?" Some people have much patience with my rambling style of telling a story. Otto does not.

"I'd better start at the beginning," I said.

"You do that."

Harry hid—or tried to hide—a smile. He always says the way I ramble I'd drive a saint to drink; he was enjoying seeing Otto bite me off in mid-phrase the way he kept doing. I was trying to start at the beginning. But with so many stories it's hard to tell where the beginning is. "There were eight kids," I said. "At least I think eight kids." I stopped, counting on my fingers and trying to remember back to my sophomore year in high school. "Well, seven or eight; I'm not sure if it was three girls or four. Audrey and Roma and Lantana—"

"Lantana?" Otto interrupted, his eyebrows raised.

"Lantana. I swear. I guess that's all. I guess it was seven, three girls and four boys. Patrick was the oldest. And Richard, and Oliver, and Harrison—they called him Sonny because he was the baby of the family. And it was short for Harrison, too, I guess."

"Okay," Otto said. There was resignation in his voice, and I suddenly realized he must feel now as I had felt trying to pry facts out of Deborah Mossberg. But he had to have this background for the rest of it to make sense, and he'd see that soon enough.

"Well, the girls all got married," I said. "Roma married this guy named Carl Gilbert, I know him a little—he was lots older than me, but one of my brothers went to school with him. He was always kind of a schlock."

"A schlock?" Otto repeated.

"Oh, you know—the kind of guy that never did anything quite wrong or quite right. Just sort of mediocre. I always thought he'd grow up to be an accountant or something like that. Anyway they finally moved away. And Audrey married somebody but I don't know who—nobody I ever met—and she moved away too. And then Lantana married Billy Jack Turner and they run Turner's Mobile Home Park."

Otto looked puzzled, but Harry nodded again. Despite the California-sounding name, Turner's is a fifties-style trailer court off Belknap, just outside the Fort Worth city limits.

"And then their parents—I've heard they used to have money before the Depression, but by the time I knew them they were just dirt farmers and dirt poor at that—died within about a year of each other. And Oliver got killed in a car wreck and Richard is an army sergeant and he's always gone to Alaska or Germany or some place like that. Or was. I guess he's retired by now but I don't know where he retired to. Anyway, that left Patrick and Sonny living here. Patrick kept the old home place."

"That's it we saw today? Where the bodies were?" Otto by now was really paying attention.

"Uh-huh. And Sonny—well, Sonny drank, and shot pool, and bowled, and—"

"None of those come free. How did he—"

"Oh. Well, I don't know. He worked as a carpenter sometimes, and he had odd jobs here and there and I think once or twice he worked a little while at some place that manufactured mobile homes. He got by. And I think he sponged off Patrick some. Patrick, by then, was a cop. A city policeman. In Fort Worth. He hadn't made any kind of rank—just a patrolman, and at that time they still had some walking beats—"

"How long ago are we talking about?" Otto interrupted.

"I don't remember for sure; I was in the tenth grade but I don't remember exactly what time of year it was, call it fifty-eight, fifty-nine, somewhere around there."

"Okay, and what happened? I think we've got enough background."

"The first thing that happened was, Patrick got married. Her name was—golly, what was it? Mary? Carrie? Something fluffy—anyway, she was a lot younger than Patrick and she was, oh, silly is the best way I can describe it. Very young, very—giddy. Remember, I was fifteen or sixteen then. And she seemed silly even to me."

"But you were always a little old for your age," Harry said. He'd been listening intently, while eating a baked potato.

"Not that old. It's just that she was awfully young for hers. She acted like a seventh-grader. And she must have been nineteen, twenty—old enough to seem ancient to me. Anyhow, Sonny—" I didn't mean to pause. But I'd been talking with my mouth full, my stomach having unaccountably decided it was hungry after all, and my mouth had gotten empty again. I reached for some more potato, and Otto took the opportunity to ask, "The old story?"

"Yeah. Basically. There was a party. On a Saturday night. A surprise birthday party for Patrick. And Sonny and—Susie, that was her name, Susie—slipped out to the grape arbor. And Patrick caught them."

"Oh? So he—"

"Not then. Then Susie went back into the house in tears and Sonny stormed off cussing and the party was over. My mother was at the party, and I remember she came home very upset."

"It takes a lot to upset your mother," Harry observed quietly.

"Yeah. But she was upset. Not so much at the situation as at the fact that they were airing it in public, so to speak. You know, the wash-your-dirty-linen-in-private sort of thing. Anyhow, I guess Patrick brooded about it. A lot. And then the next Monday he came in off patrol about the middle of his shift. He told his sergeant he was sick, and he took off his uniform and put on his jeans and T-shirt and said he was going home, but instead he went off hunting his brother. He found him late that afternoon, in front of Shiloh Baptist Church, while there was some kind of youth activity going on. There were kids all over the place. But Patrick didn't care. I guess—I guess he was counting on the so-called unwritten law to save him. And it might have done it, if it had happened on Saturday night." I stopped to think about it a little. What I hadn't told Otto, what I wasn't going to unless it became absolutely necessary, was that I had been one of those kids.

There may be more than one Shiloh Baptist Church in Fort Worth. I don't know about that; I don't very often get calls to churches. But the one I went to was a little white asbestos-sided building that was then outside the city limits of Forth Worth. It's just barely inside now, but it's still a rural area.

I saw that killing. Even now, after more than sixteen

years in law enforcement, I remember it vividly, but not as vividly as I might have, because to me, then, it wasn't quite real. People—people I knew, brothers to each other—don't stand in the green grass in front of a church and shout profanities at each other until one of them hauls out a revolver and shoots the other once in the chest, and the other spins to his left with a leg twisted grotesquely in front of him and an unbelieving look on his face, and then falls on his left side with blood bubbling out of his mouth and lies still—still— still while the other brother runs toward him yelling, "Sonny, Sonny, I didn't mean—" while someone somewhere is screaming.

Things like that don't happen, not in front of fifteen-year-old girls, and so of course it didn't happen, and in a minute Sonny would get up and laugh—he was always a practical joker—and Patrick would laugh too and that would be the end of it.

Only my Sunday school teacher, hearing the someone screaming who was me, came and took me away before Sonny got up and laughed.

"He shot his brother." Otto's voice was quiet. "Then what happened?"

I shrugged. "There were a lot of hard feelings in town. Sonny, oddly enough, was more popular than Patrick, although in retrospect I guess Sonny just about wasn't worth killing. I say 'in town' but of course I mean in our part of town. But all the same there were more hard feelings than anybody needed. There was even some lynch talk. They decided Patrick might not be safe in the Tarrant County jail and they moved him over to Dallas; that's how much talk there was. And I remember my father said when Patrick got out of prison he better not ever come back to Tarrant County. He said there were enough people still mad that he might get strung up to the nearest mesquite tree."

"What was he actually convicted of?" Harry asked. He was four years ahead of me in high school; he was in the Marine Corps by the time that happened, and he may not ever have gotten a straight story. And historically, Texas courts have been extremely lenient toward men who have reacted violently to being cuckolded.

"I don't know. That's one of the things I need to find out."

My plate had unaccountably become empty. Feeling much better, I crossed my arms on the table and looked at Otto. "Now, you wanted to know what I was going to do."

"I did and I do."

"Monday I'm going to get into old records and find out what Kelly was convicted of, and what prison he went to, and how long ago he was released, and who knew him while he was there, and—"

"Why are you going to do that?"

Was he serious? That was about as obvious as anything had ever been to me in my professional life. "Because it is perfectly clear that Kelly was killed by a criminal associate, and most likely that same person was the one who shot Bassinger."

"That makes sense," Otto admitted.

"Now what are you going to do?" I asked.

Otto grinned slowly. "I'm following the same track. The ransom was mailed. That's all French has been willing to say, yet, that he mailed it. I've got to get him to tell me where he mailed it, what address, and I'll lay you even odds that it went to the Kelly farm."

"So you've got to talk to him."

"Yeah. And I've got to get him to talk to me, which may be harder."

That wasn't a job I'd want. But in the end, of course, I got it.

He was in the Fort Worth Police Station at seven o'clock on Sunday morning, wanting to talk to the detective on the case, and when a dispatcher called me I went on and called Otto. There was no sense in having him provide the same information twice, to each of us separately, and if we were both working on the same end then we'd have a lot of the same questions to ask.

He was sitting in a small interview room when I arrived, and Otto was standing in the hall. He'd waited for me to get there, after one of the secretaries—there are two on duty on Sunday—told him she'd put Mr. French into the small room because he seemed awfully distraught.

I opened the door, but Otto was right behind me.

French was a big man, fleshy with solidity clothing big bones. He had a shock of light brown hair, bright blue eyes, and what would probably, under normal conditions, be an open, friendly face. He would look bluff, hearty, almost the stereotypical back-slapping salesman, except for something a little deeper about him that was hard to define. That would be his normal appearance. Today he seemed shocked, bewildered, not quite comprehending.

Predictably he looked at Otto first. "I'm Jared French," he said, automatically standing and extending his hand as habit took control.

"Mr. French, I'm Otto Castillo. I'm the postal inspector assigned to the case. This is Deb Ralston with the Fort Worth Police Department."

"Mr. French," I said, and waited for his reaction. If

he was going to ask for a man detective, I would try to talk Captain Millner into getting one.

But he didn't. His expression was as close to a smile as it was likely to get for a while. "A woman detective. She'd—Helen—would like that. She always used to ask for a woman doctor. When we had to take her into the emergency room—which we did so often—she'd be indignant if she couldn't have a woman doctor." As fast as it had come, the near smile faded. "My doctor wouldn't let me come out last night; my wife was—upset. Very upset. Who found her? I want to know that first. I want to thank—"

"Both of us found her," I said.

"In an old farmhouse?"

"That's right."

"How did you know to look there?"

"We didn't. We were on a different case."

"A different—?"

"They're almost certainly interrelated," Otto told him, and explained, somewhat more crisply than I would have done. At one point during the explanation, French sat again, rather limply, in an old wooden armchair. There was utter silence in the room when Otto finally stopped talking.

Then French took a deep breath. "So he killed Helen so she couldn't identify him. Then he killed his accomplice so he could have all the money for himself. Then he burned the car so—so—for some reason or other—then he killed the postman because the postman saw him burning the car."

"Maybe," Otto said.

"What do you mean, maybe? You know—"

"We don't know who killed Helen and we don't know exactly why, although you may be right that it was to

· 49 ·

prevent identification. We don't know for sure whether Kelly was even involved in the kidnapping, just that his farm was. And we don't know who killed him or why. As you surmised, we don't have any idea at all why the car was burned. And although you're probably right about why the mail carrier was killed, that's not certain either."

"What are you doing to try to find out? About all of it, I mean."

"Everything we can. Believe me, everything we can. But we need to ask some questions—"

"I want to go see Helen first. Can't I go see her now?"

"I'm sorry, but that's not possible," I told him, as gently as I could.

"What do you mean, not possible?"

Otto didn't see as much need for gentleness. He glanced at the clock. "The autopsy's scheduled for—"

"I haven't consented to any—" French's face had crumpled in disbelief, and his voice was rising.

"Mr. French." I kept my voice as low-pitched as I could; sometimes that helps to calm people. "In this type of situation, no consent from the family is required. An autopsy is necessary and it is performed. You certainly should have been notified, however, and I'm going to find out why you weren't. But as Mr. Castillo told you, right now it's in progress. That's why you can't see her now. They'll call me, here, when it's through. But—I did see her. And you don't want to. Honestly. You don't want to. If it were my child—" I left the sentence unfinished.

"Your child—do you have any children?" French saw, in a glance, what Otto still hadn't noticed. "I mean any others—besides that one?"

"Three. And I can't really say I know how you feel, because I don't. But I can say that you shouldn't see Helen's body now."

French took a deep breath. "What—what did they do to her?"

That was a question I couldn't answer. "I don't know." That wasn't much of an answer, even if it was the only one I had.

"You couldn't—"

His voice was bewildered, and Otto, still standing behind me, said, "It had been a while, Mr. French. And we don't know how long a while."

"She'd been missing for a week," French said, and then he started to cry. I turned and shut the door of the little room, and Otto looked uneasy. The kinds of cases that postal inspectors work don't, I suppose, so often involve weeping victims and weeping relatives of victims.

Finally French stopped crying and said, "You wanted to ask me some questions. How will that help?"

"It might help us to catch them," I said. "Information from you—"

"What good will catching them do Helen?"

"None at all," I agreed. "But it might keep them from doing the same thing to somebody else's child. Do you feel like talking now, or should we wait?"

"I'll answer your questions. If it'll help. Besides, I want to wait here till—till your call comes in. So ask away."

"Can you remember exactly where you mailed the ransom?" Otto asked. That, to me as well as to him, bespoke an incredible stupidity on the part of both the kidnappers and French. For if French had reported the kidnapping at once, as he should have had sense enough to do, federal agents would have accompanied the package every inch of the way through the mails, smoothly picking up at least one of the conspirators when the package was delivered.

And the kidnappers, ordering the package mailed, should have expected that result.

But French waited three days after mailing the package before notifying the police. And even then, clinging still to the hopeless belief that Helen would be returned alive, he had refused to tell the mailing address; the anonymous voice on the telephone had said that if police came in Helen would be shot. That much we had gotten from the FBI agents Saturday afternoon.

French, in a flat voice, gave the route number. "Box Two-twenty–J, Fort Worth, Texas," he added. "I don't remember the zip. They told me not to write the address down anywhere but on the mailing label. I didn't. But I remembered. All but the zip. I don't remember the zip."

"I don't need the zip," Otto said, glancing at me significantly. "What did it look like? The package?"

"It was a boot box. A cardboard box I'd bought boots in. Tony Lamas, the boots were Tony Lamas. Twenty-five-hundred hundred-dollar bills."

"You got them out of your bank? New bills or old?"

"Old. I called the bank. They said it'd take about a day to get them together. It did."

"What bank?"

He told us. It was a big bank in Dallas. Somebody there should have realized two hundred and fifty thousand dollars in old hundred-dollar bills was either ransom money or a drug buy. Most likely somebody did, and figured it was none of his—or her—business.

"Did you write the serial numbers down?"

A long silence. "They told me not to."

"So you didn't."

"I didn't. No, I didn't."

"So you had the money and you had the boot box. Then what did you do?"

"I counted it again, to be sure it was the right amount of money, in case somebody had made a mistake. But they hadn't. Then I put the money in the boot box and I taped it shut and I wrapped it in brown wrapping paper and I wrote the address with a black Marksalot and I put tape over the address so it wouldn't run if it rained and I took the package to the post office and I mailed it."

"Which post office?"

"It's close to where I used to live. On—on—I don't remember the name of the street. Off Alpha Road. Kind of behind Valley View Mall."

I don't know Dallas all that well, but Otto nodded. The description clearly meant something to him. "The wrapping paper. Was it regular wrapping paper, or did you cut up a grocery sack?"

I couldn't imagine what he was getting at with that question. Anybody who could pay that kind of ransom could afford wrapping paper, but of course people have quirks. Anyway, what difference did it make?

French didn't ask that. "It was regular wrapping paper."

"Do you have the rest of the roll left?"

"It wasn't a roll. It was a single sheet. I bought it at the drugstore."

"What drugstore?"

French told him.

"Do you have the wrapper it came in around the house somewhere?"

"I threw it away."

"Do you remember the brand?"

"Uh-uh."

"The address. Did you write it or print it?"

"Printed it."

"With a black marker, you said?"

"What?"

"You said you printed the address with a black marker?"

"Oh. Yeah. A black Marksalot."

"Do you still have it?"

"No, I threw it away. In the post office, I threw it in the trash barrel at the—post office—"

He was going to cry again. Otto ignored that.

"If I got you a sheet of brown paper and a black marker, would you show me how you printed it, the best you can remember?"

"I can do it, but why?"

"So I'll have something to show some of the people who might have seen the package."

"Oh. Yeah. Okay."

Otto headed for the main office of the detective bureau, leaving the door of the interview room open, and French stared bleakly at the wall. While Otto was firing machine-gun questions at him, he didn't have much time to think about their import; now he was thinking again, and his thoughts weren't—judging from his expression as well as from the situation—good ones. So it was as much out of mercy as out of need to know that I began to ask questions while Otto was out of the room. "Do you know a Patrick Kelly?"

"No. But I could have met him. I meet probably several hundred people a month. I don't remember them. I don't remember anybody named Patrick Kelly. I know some Kellys but I don't know anybody at all named Patrick, at least not to say I know him. I must have met some Patricks but—are you a Mormon?"

"A what?" I was mentally shifting gears at that unexpected question.

"A Mormon. Are you a Mormon?"

"No, why?"

"I am. And you look familiar. I thought I might have met you at some regional conference or something."

"No, I've never been to one. But my son has started going to the Mormon church. He plays basketball, and I've been to a few of his games. Maybe—"

"How old is your son?"

"Fifteen—sixteen. He just turned sixteen a couple of months ago. He was still fifteen last basketball season."

"That must have been it then. My boy Randy plays basketball in the church leagues. And he was fifteen last basketball season too. What's your boy's name?"

I told him, and he shook his head. "That doesn't ring a bell. I mean, I remember a kid with that name, but he looked oriental. Long tall drink of water."

"That's Hal," I agreed. "We don't know anything at all about his natural father, but we figure he must have been tall."

"Oh, he's adopted."

"All my children are adopted."

"Except that one."

"Except that one," I agreed, figuring I might as well get used to having attention paid to my midsection.

"Why'd—that's none of my business, is it?"

"Why'd I wait so long before becoming pregnant? It sure wasn't my idea. Or my husband's. Anyway, we need to get back to—"

French wasn't ready to get back to the subject at

hand. "The reason I wanted to know was, I've been thinking lately, in some ways it handicaps us."

"What does?" He had me totally lost.

"Just—you spend so much time with your church. Even when you're at school you're at church, in a way, because in high school we've got this thing called seminary." I nodded; I was well acquainted with seminary. It involved Hal, on the approximately three out of five days he remembered to get up in time, stumbling out the front door at 5:00 A.M. to catch his ride, and banging back in at seven to tell Harry and me many things we did not want to know.

What I could not understand was what seminary had to do with being handicapped.

French went on talking. "You grow up with ideas of honor. And right behavior. And people don't hurt people. And—and then you get out into the real world and you find out people don't do what you've been taught is right and people do lie to people and people do hurt people. Only—only you don't really learn it at all. I couldn't—really—believe they would hurt Helen. Even after they kidnapped her, I—I was almost sorry for them, anybody that wanted money so bad he'd use a child to get it. But I think—I think I really expected they'd give Helen back. They wouldn't really hurt children because people don't hurt children. Because—because in our church people don't hurt children."

"In any church, Mr. French. I grew up a Baptist. My husband grew up a Presbyterian. You're talking about the difference between righteous people and evil people. If you grow up around righteous people you expect everybody to be righteous, if that's not too old-fashioned a word. And if expecting people to act right is being handicapped, then long live handicaps. The only thing is, you need to know that not everybody is going to act the way you've been taught to act."

"And that's what I didn't learn. I should have." He started talking about a series of forgeries and bombings in Salt Lake City, and he was still talking when Otto came back.

Then French made a replica of the package, as well as he could, and I telephoned the medical examiner's office and found out the autopsy had been put off until afternoon for some reason nobody could explain to me.

So I told French and he went to a motel in Fort Worth—not all the way back to Dallas—and said he'd be back up to the police station later.

After he left, Otto stood up. "Come on," he said.

Hoisting myself up from my chair, I asked, "Come on where?"

"Back out to the scene. There's something I want a look at."

"That's what I thought," Otto muttered.

"That's what you thought about what?" I asked. And then I saw what he was looking at.

We were in a postal inspection service car, parked on the dusty shoulder of Four Mile Road, looking at a bank of mailboxes nailed to a two-by-four supported by two splintered old creosote posts. There were nine boxes in the bank: Box 220-A through Box 220-I. Most of them had names scrawled on them in fading black paint.

There was no Box 220-J.

There had been; there was room on the post for a tenth box, but dark bent nails and rust streaks showed where it had been removed long ago.

And one new gray aluminum nail, driven up at an

angle through the two-by-four, its point protruding into the air, told a different story.

"They put a box on just long enough to get the package. Then they removed it again."

"But why remove it?" I wondered. "That doesn't make a whole lot of sense."

"Somebody would know it didn't belong . . . Cooper. Cooper?"

"What?"

"The mail carrier on that route. Isn't his name Cooper? Damn it, I wrote it down somewhere." Otto had begun rummaging through a notebook he took out of his pocket.

"How in the world should I know?"

"Sorry. I was thinking out loud."

"But how could anybody be so utterly stupid?" I asked. "I mean, taking the box away doesn't change anything. It's Box Two-twenty. All this is Box Two-twenty. Taking the box lettered J away doesn't change anything. Whenever French gave up waiting and reported the kidnapping, he'd remember that, and all anybody would have to do is come out here and start looking and you'd find the farmhouse in half an hour at the most. So—"

"So maybe Kelly wasn't in it," Otto said. "Because there's no way Kelly could disassociate himself from the address. So maybe Kelly was a victim too. Maybe we were supposed to find Kelly and assume he did it and not look any farther—"

"Oh, come on, Otto! He was murdered! There's no way that could stop us from looking!"

"Well, that's true," Otto agreed reluctantly.

But I am well known—or maybe I should say notorious—for my hunches, and this time my brain had gone into high gear. "Except I'm not so sure he was murdered," I said.

Otto stared at me. "What in the world are you talking about? You know damn well he was murdered."

"No, I just know that he was shot. I'm not sure he was murdered. It's possible—"

"What's possible? That he shot Bassinger and then hared back to the house and committed suicide? Not unless he ate the shotgun he didn't. Anyway, he was dead at least a full day before Bassinger. So what in the hell are you talking about?"

"I'm thinking out loud," I said, tossing Otto's own phrase back at him. "This thing is looking awfully funny to me. No, I don't think he committed suicide. I'm thinking more along the lines of an accident. Let's go on up to the house."

The black and white police car parked on the tarred road blocked the driveway, but nobody was visible in the car or in the yard. The dog, curled on the front porch, raised its head and then stood up and trotted toward us, nodding its head and wagging from the shoulders back just the way my dog Pat does. It rubbed its head against Otto's shin and Otto, looking embarrassed, said, "Hello, dog. Thirsty again?"

No, the water pan was full and kibbled dog food was spilled on the wooden porch. "Maybe he just likes you," I said with deliberate malice. Otto's dislike for dogs is well known.

The dog, glossy black except for its tan eyebrows and tan vest, looked back and barked once, sharply.

I glanced from the dog to the house, to the open door of the house. The door that shouldn't be open. The front porch that was empty of Patrolman Bill Livingston, who was supposed to be guarding the scene.

"Bill!" I shouted, and started to lope toward the house, listening for an answering shout that didn't come.

Otto said, "Oh, shit!" and took off in a run, passing me in approximately three strides, and I started running to try to catch up with him.

Which I managed to do, but only because he stumbled on the bottom stair.

Bill Livingston was sprawled facedown in the front hall, his sandy blond hair dull with drying blood that spread in a puddle around him. His labored breathing rattled the old pine floor. I grabbed the walkie-talkie that lay just beyond his outstretched right hand. "Headquarters, do you read me?"

· 4 ·

"At seven. you know what time my shift starts."

"You came on duty at seven. Why didn't you check on Livingston? You knew he was out there at the Kelly place." Sergeant Ben Isaacs was in charge of day watch, dispatch. The dispatcher he'd hauled into the detective bureau, Karen Mayfield, looked very badly frightened, as well she might with detectives, intelligence officers, and a postal inspector, as well as her own supervisor, all hovering around her.

But frightened or not, she stood her ground. "No, sir, I—"

"You what?"

"Give the girl time to breathe," Captain Millner drawled.

She glanced at him gratefully and then turned back to Sergeant Isaacs. "I didn't know he was out there."

"Why didn't you know? You're supposed to know where—"

"Look," Karen said, her voice shaking, "I get a log of everybody who's supposed to be on duty in narcotics, intelligence, and stakeout, and I guarantee you I know where every one of them is all the time. But Bill Livingston wasn't on that log. As far as I could tell from the watch bills, Livingston was on three to eleven, uniform division. Now how was I supposed to know—"

The days of "the dispatcher" are long gone, in a city the size of Fort Worth. We have banks of dispatchers, answering telephones, doing things with computers, listening to radios, talking on radios, and most important, keeping track of where who is when. But only one dispatcher per shift has the primary duty of keeping track of the special radio frequency used by people working at least semiundercover. Karen was one of those dispatchers.

"Who dispatched eleven to seven?" Isaacs demanded. "That's who should have told you. Vinson, wasn't it supposed to be Vinson?"

"Yes, sir, I mean, no, sir—"

"Didn't I have Vinson scheduled for—"

"Vinson was scheduled but he was competing in a race and he couldn't get back in time because the race started later than it was supposed to and he called in and got hold of the patrol sergeant and the patrol sergeant said he shouldn't take the day off at the last minute like that but under the circumstances if he couldn't get back he couldn't get back and there wasn't much use—"

"Wait a minute," Isaacs interrupted. "This is Vinson we're talking about. Greg Vinson. The guy that—"

"It was a wheelchair race," I interrupted. "I knew he was going to be in it. He'd been telling me about it. But it was supposed to be over in time for—"

"Well, it wasn't over," Karen said firmly. "It started late. So it took longer. Look, Vinson's good. I betcha he makes it to the Olympics if—"

"Karen, I think it will be absolutely super peachy-keen if our paraplegic dispatcher makes it to the wheel-chair races in the Olympics. I will be absolutely positively tickled to death, okay? I hope he gets a gold medal. I hope he gets three gold medals. I hope he gets a dozen gold medals. But right now I am not one damn bit interested in the race. Right now I am trying to find out how long Corporal Bill Livingston was lying uncon-scious on the floor of the Kelly farmhouse, and why the hell none of my dispatchers knew it. Now if Vinson wasn't on duty then, who—"

"Oh. Oh, well, nobody could get ahold of you and the sergeant that had morning watch was out of town and so the patrol sergeant—"

"Don't tell me standard operating procedure. I wrote it. Just tell me what happened."

"They called my mother to see if I wanted some over-time, and—"

"Karen, I said—"

"I'm getting to that. The patrol sergeant told my mom he was pretty desperate, because just about every dis-patcher he'd called was unavailable for one reason or another and the two that weren't were still trainees. Look, I would have come on in only I couldn't because I was in Dallas."

"In Dallas."

"Yeah. I wanted to see Gr—to see Vinson race. I fig-ured somebody from the department ought to."

"Oh, ho," Isaacs said softly. "So Cupid flies through the dispatch room."

Her face reddening, her eyes defiant, Karen said, "Yes. And so I went to see him race."

"Well, he's a fine young fellow," Isaacs said, "and it's a damn shame he went and hot-rodded that motorcycle. But you're a young woman; what good'll he do you—"

Her face even redder, Karen said, "That's none of your particular business, is it, sergeant?"

"I suppose it isn't," Isaacs agreed. "I suppose it isn't. Okay, you weren't there so you didn't go in. Do you know who actually did dispatch eleven to seven?"

That was a stupid question for two reasons. First, Karen obviously knew who she'd relieved, and second, a glance at the logs would answer the question.

But we didn't need to look at the logs. "Shea. Patrolman Shea," Karen was saying. "The sergeant told my mom if I couldn't come in he was going to have to be scraping the bottom of the barrel, but there were a couple of patrol officers who'd had dispatch experience when they were hurt and couldn't patrol, so he'd call one of—" She broke off, staring at our faces. "What's wrong?"

"How long have you been with this department, Karen?" I asked. "About four months?"

"About. Why?"

"Let's just say Danny Shea is not scraping the bottom of the barrel," Isaacs told her. "Shea is what you get if you move the barrel and look under it, and if this doesn't get him fired nothing ever will. Okay, in that case it wasn't your fault. Who's filling in for you right now, Rose? Go tell her you'll take it back. No, wait, before you do that go bring me a copy of the log from— Deb, what time?"

"He went to Four Mile Road about one-thirty and sat on the mail truck till about eight. Then he took over the

· 64 ·

house. He was actually off duty by then but there were a couple of the regular stakeout people on leave, and he was going to sit on it till I got back out there this morning."

"The log from three o'clock on, the beginning of Duncan's shift," Isaacs said. "I want to find out if he reported anything at all, to Duncan or to Shea."

"I've got a lab crew flying in from Memphis," Otto told me.

"What do you plan on having them do?" I asked.

"What are you talking about?" demanded Inspector McMurray. I'd just met him; he was Otto's boss, and I hadn't quite figured out yet whether he was the actual head of the Fort Worth regional office of the Postal Inspection Service, or whether he was just some kind of squad leader.

"We've already worked the crime scene," I said. "By 'we' of course I mean our ident unit."

"Without my authorization?" McMurray was swelling up like a pouter pigeon.

"What do you want a lab crew to do?" I asked again. "Look, McMurray, I'm serious. Did Otto tell you exactly what we have there? Fingerprint evidence? There is no reason whatsoever for the killer ever to have touched, or even approached, the truck; that shot was fired from about seven feet away, but just in case he did we dusted it anyway. Firearms evidence? Shotgun. No ejected shell; I looked and so did Otto and so did our crime scene people. He must have picked it up and taken it with him. Evidence on the ground? What evidence do you expect to find on the ground after the ground was stirred up by an airplane, two police cars, a postal inspector's car, and a fire truck? What's that likely to leave? Photography? We took pictures and the medical examiner's investigator took pictures. We've got all the pictures you want. So what do you want the lab to do? Work the arson? Sorry, it's not your case. Work a kidnapping and murder? That's not your case either. So if you want your lab team to come in from Memphis let them come right ahead, but I say again, I don't know what you expect them to do when they get here."

"And that's that," Otto Castillo said. "Sorry, boss, she's right and I should have thought of—keep your hands off that."

"Huh?" McMurray looked down at the envelope he was carelessly holding.

"Oh well, I don't guess it matters. I was thinking fingerprints but of course they never got it. But damn it, man, don't you know not to walk into somebody's office and start handling evidence?"

"That's evidence? It looks to me like advertising."

It was a white business envelope with the blue logo of French's Chevrolets in the upper left corner; it was addressed, in blue ink, in sprawling masculine hand-writing, to the same box the ransom had gone to.

"It's evidence in a kidnapping," I told him.

"As I believe somebody just reminded me, the post office doesn't work kidnappings." McMurray's tone was sardonic. He knew as well as I did, if not better, that anything that went through the mails was post office business, no matter who had original jurisdiction in the crime.

"About a hundred percent certain whoever pulled the kidnapping shot Bassinger," Castillo said.

"You got authorization from the sending end to open it, or do we need a search warrant?" He turned to me, rather condescendingly. "You know live mail—"

"I know you can't touch live mail without a warrant or consent from one end of the line," I said. "I'm trying to locate the man who mailed it. We—Otto and I—were talking to him this morning, but we didn't know about this then."

"Okay," McMurray said. "Is all of this evidence in the kidnapping?" His hand gesture indicated several bags of mail sitting in Castillo's office, piled around the chair in which I was sitting.

"Uh-uh," Castillo said. "It's just undelivered mail, what was in Bassinger's truck. I doubt any of it means anything to the investigation. It tells us where he got to on the deliveries, but we knew where he got to because we know where he was found. He wasn't shot for the mail on the truck; he was shot because he walked in on an arson, and it seems—as we've been saying—about a hundred percent certain the arson was related to the kidnap-murder. The question is, why'd he walk in on the arson? What was he doing there? It wasn't on his route. But I think this is the answer." He took the envelope out of McMurray's hand and tapped it on the table.

"Explain," McMurray said.

"He was on a dead-end road," I said. "There aren't any mailboxes on that road. So why was he there?" Castillo glanced at me; we'd spent some time talking this out before McMurray came in. "We think this is why. We think he knew who Box Two-twenty-J belonged to, and since the box was gone he figured he'd just front-door deliver it. He didn't have to, of course, but he was that kind of man; he was conscientious. And he'd been on that route fifty years."

"Meaning?"

"Fifty years ago Joe Kelly was alive," I said.

"Joe Kelly?"

"Not important now," Castillo said. "Just, he knew who Box Two-twenty-J belonged to."

"And that says to us," I went on, "that somebody set Patrick Kelly up, and whoever it was, it's the same person killed Bassinger. Kelly was set up to take the rap, before the whole thing started going wrong. We don't think he meant to kill Kelly." At least I didn't think that; we'd argued about it, but Castillo didn't interrupt me now. "But if he didn't, then why was he so sure that Kelly wouldn't squeal on him?" That's what didn't make sense; that's why Castillo and I had argued about the whole theory.

"Give me some background," McMurray suggested, and as Castillo started giving background I slipped into another office to try to call Jared French again and get him over to the federal building.

"Open it," Jared French said. "Why would I care if you open it?"

He'd been crying; that was easy to tell because the whites of his blue eyes were reddened and his whole face was swollen. But he had himself under control now, and he added, "You might as well open it. There's nothing in there. I—it was just—I remembered the address, and I had sent what they asked for and Helen wasn't back and so I wrote them again: Did they get it? Was that why they killed Helen, because I remembered the address when they'd told me not to?"

"No, Mr. French, they never got the letter," Castillo told him. "That didn't have anything to do with her death. Here, if you'll just sign this—"

A belated caution took over, and French paused with the pen in his hand. "What am I signing?"

"Permission for us to open the letter," Castillo said, as patiently as he could.

"Yeah?" French said in a puzzled tone. "I thought you guys could open any mail you wanted to."

"You thought wrong." French probably couldn't hear the impatience in Castillo's voice, but I could; I'd known Castillo several years. "What we can and can't do is set out in the law. And we can't open mail without a search warrant, unless either the person who mailed it or the person who was supposed to get it gives written consent."

"Okay. I sure didn't know that." French signed the form, and Castillo opened the letter. He skimmed it and handed it to me.

French, who had been watching us, asked huskily, "Is it okay if I have it back?"

Castillo glanced at me, and I said, "I wish we could return it. But right now—"

"Why? I don't understand. If they never got it—"

"Because we think that's why the postman was where he was. We think he was on his way to deliver this letter. You see, this was going to a box near the end of his route, but the box itself was gone."

"Gone?"

"That's right. It had been removed. And instead of sending the letter back to you he apparently decided he'd just take a short drive over to the farm the box belonged to and leave the letter there."

"And that was where—"

"That was where he was killed. Yes."

"So an old man died because I wrote a letter I should've had sense enough not to write."

This time Castillo didn't let me answer. "Yeah," he said. "He was killed because you cared about your daughter. He was killed because he cared about getting his work done right, not half-assed, so he took a trip he didn't have to make. For cryin' out loud, French, don't take off on a guilt trip. He was killed because some son of a bitch decided to shoot him, that's why he was killed, not because of anything you did or he did or any other decent normal human being did. He was killed because some son of a bitch cared more about money than about human life, and all any of us can do about that kind of person is try to catch him and cage him so he can't do anything else."

French stared at Castillo, stared with a kind of blind numbness that had to be the result of the shock he'd been drifting in and out of. Then finally he shook his head and said, "Yeah. You're right. Of course you're right. It's just that—something like this—you keep thinking there must have been something I could have done that I didn't think of."

"There wasn't," I told him. "There really wasn't." And that was almost certainly true. Yes, he could—and should—have called the police a lot sooner than he did, but most likely that wouldn't have saved Helen. Killers kill because they're killers.

French had to be persuaded to leave the office so that we could get on about our business. But at the moment there didn't seem to be a very good way to go at getting him to leave. He continued to stare at Castillo for a minute longer; then he shook his head like a man rising out of deep water and asked, "How did she die? Does anybody even know that yet?"

"I'll check," I said, and reached for the telephone.

Yes, the autopsy—which the medical examiner's office prefers to call a postmortem examination—had been completed, and Rose Sprague, the secretary, gave me the gist of the report she was in the middle of typing. It appeared that Helen had died in the trunk of a car—at least she had been in the trunk of a car at or near the time she died. Her bronchial passages and lungs contained tiny amounts of rubber, fiber, traces of brake fluid, traces of oil. There was a small amount of carbon monoxide in her bloodstream, indicating that the car was moving, but it wasn't nearly enough to cause death.

In fact, there was no apparent cause of death. It might have resulted from suffocation and then again it might not. If it had there was no apparent reason why, as there were no signs of manual suffocation, and most car trunks let enough air in. Of course it would have been hot in the trunk, but this time of year it shouldn't have been too hot for life.

I relayed the information as unemotionally as I could. French was torn up enough; it wouldn't do any good for me to get emotional too. I kept reminding myself of that, as I tried not to see his face.

His voice sounding more tired now than anything else, French said, "Yeah, well, you know she had asthma real bad; she had to carry an inhaler thing around with her all the time, that's why she carried a purse as young as she was. If she couldn't get at it—you know emotion brings attacks on—seems like every Christmas, every birthday party she'd wind up in the emergency room, so being stuck in the trunk of a car—" quite suddenly he was crying again.

"Oh, shit," Castillo said loudly, then hastily apologized. "Mr. French, I'm sorry, it's just when I think of a son of a bitch like that—"

"You can't bring her back," French said.

"No, but maybe we can stop the bastard from stuffing some other little girl in the trunk of a car," Castillo said. "We've got to get on to work. Mr. French, I'd suggest you go on back to your motel room and get some rest and then head on back to Dallas."

"I want to stay here."

"Why?" I asked.

He stared at me. "Why? Well, I—"

"Where's your wife? Your other children?"

"In Dallas. But—"

"If it were my child I'd want my husband with me," I said. "Not in another town where there wasn't anything for him to do anyway."

"But I've got to take—her—back to Dallas."

"You can't. You ought to know—"

I took a deep breath and headed out onto shaky theological grounds, wishing now I had listened more to Hal when he came in all excited telling me things I didn't want to know. "You ought to know that's not Helen; that's just Helen's body. Helen's somewhere else and she's okay."

French drew a long, shaky breath. "I know. But—"

"The body has to be transported in a hearse, in a sealed casket. You can't take it anywhere."

"All right," French said. He blew his nose on a pocket handkerchief, stuffed it back into his pocket, stared at me, stared at Castillo, solemnly shook hands with both of us, and walked out the door.

Castillo put French's letter into a folder and closed the drawer on it, picked up his clipboard, and stood up. And Assistant Postmaster Don Goslin walked in the door.

"Where were you?" Castillo asked, and sat down again.

"We had an Elks convention in Arlington."

"Gee, such a long way off," Castillo said.

"Knock it off, Castillo," Goslin said. "The idiots forgot

where I was. I told 'em but they forgot, and so nobody got in touch with me. I didn't know until I got a look at the Sunday paper. What the hell happened?"

"You read it in the paper," Castillo said.

"Now look ahere—"

"The report in the paper was pretty accurate," I interrupted. "There's not much to add to it yet but bits and pieces of investigation and none of those bits and pieces fit together yet."

"Damn," Goslin said. "You know, I been knowing Roy thirty years. He—was—s'posed to be at the convention too. I told him to forget about the route, let one of the young substitutes take it, and he said no, he'd finish it up and then head for Arlington, said he wouldn't miss much doing that. I—we were having a ritual contest. And he was on the ritual team, and he didn't show up for practice Saturday night and our team wound up disqualified and everybody was good and mad at him. And to think of him dead—damn! We should have realized Roy would never just not show up."

There are, I should mention, several different Elks Lodges in the metro Fort Worth area. I was vaguely aware of the convention in Arlington, although we didn't go to it; Goslin I didn't know at all. I could only assume he was in a different lodge from the one Harry was in, the big one on White Settlement Road.

"Okay," said Castillo impatiently, "are we going to sit around here and hold a wake in honor of the dear departed, or are we going to get out and find out what happened to him?"

"We know what happened to him," Goslin said, looking puzzled.

"All right, then, *who* happened to him. Goslin, I'm

trying to say, get out of here so we can work . . . wait a minute. Who was the regular on the route Bassinger was filling in? Was it Cooper?"

"Well, yeah—"

"Then that's something you can do. Get Cooper up here."

"It's Sunday," Goslin protested.

"What the hell does that have to do with anything?" Castillo demanded. "Can you get Cooper up here?"

"Well, I don't know if—"

"Would you try?" I asked, trying to sound as coaxing as possible to counteract the fury in Castillo's tone. "Will you go to your office and call him and come back here and tell us if you got him and if he's going to show up here today?"

"If he doesn't make it today," Castillo added, "of course I'll have to talk with him tomorrow morning when he's supposed to be sorting."

"But that'll slow—"

"Exactly. That'll slow mail delivery and you'll get a lot of phone calls. So maybe you'd better get him on up here, okay?"

Goslin, looking puzzled, departed, and Castillo made an indescribable noise sort of akin to *gaaaa*. "He was a political appointee back in the days when all you needed to work for the post office was to vote the right ticket and get a lot of other people to do the same."

"Does that mean he's stupid?" I asked.

"It means he's stupid. Oh, hell, I shouldn't have shouted at him, though. That makes about as much sense as shouting at a mule for being a mule. He can't help being stupid. He was born that way. Ignorance can be cured. Stupidity can't. I just hope he manages to get Cooper up here and doesn't forget what I sent him to do."

"How does he manage to get the mail delivered?"

"He doesn't. Why do you think they keep shunting him off to the smallest substation they can find to put him in? And every so often the postmaster has to send somebody out to untangle, even so. If he doesn't retire pretty soon, they're going to find a way to have him presiding over a post office window at a country grocery store or something. And I suppose he'd find some way to mess even *that* up. Oh, hell, let's get to work."

But as he was gathering scattered papers into his briefcase, Goslin came back in with the surprising news that he'd reached Cooper. "Coop said he'll be here at two o'clock," he added.

Two o'clock, and it was twelve-thirty now. "You got stuff of your own to do, Deb? I'll meet you back here at one-forty-five then."

He was being surprisingly nice about working with me, once he'd gotten over his initial objection. That helped. And he hadn't made any snide comments about my midsection. He had to have noticed by now, so apparently he'd just decided saying anything wouldn't do any good.

I didn't know what he was going to be doing. I called the hospital, to be told Livingston was in surgery, and then I decided to take the time to go over to Turner's Mobile Home Park to talk with Lantana Turner. Who had been Lantana Kelly. Who was the youngest sister of Patrick Kelly, who was dead in our morgue from a shotgun blast to the face. That was confirmed now, quite easily, by fingerprint records.

It wasn't that Lantana hadn't heard her brother was dead; she had. What she hadn't heard was how long he had been dead before he was found, and she started crying when I told her that, with her head hanging over the arm of the couch. Billy Jack was watching her stoically from the yellow vinyl and metal kitchen chair he was sitting on backward with his chin on the top of the backrest.

They were a good match, Lantana and Billy Jack. Lantana was my age or thereabouts; she'd fallen behind me by high school because the Kellys weren't much on education, but I remembered her from the second grade, a lean gawky girl taller than I was, who somehow always smelled of yeast. She was, at the most, forty-three. She looked sixty. She had been slender in high school; now she was skinny, with straight stringy hair that was a sadly faded brown. She was surface clean, but her complexion had the look of ground-in ineradicable dirt that made her seem grayish in some indefinable way, and her old pinched blue eyes looked as though they needed glasses. She was wearing a mustard yellow poylester knit skirt that was stained with something like tomato juice, a bright yellow and black print blouse I vaguely remembered seeing in Lerner's two years ago—it clashed horribly with the skirt—and puce plastic shoes of the kind that are called jellies.

Billy Jack, whom I didn't remember from school, was probably five inches shorter than Lantana, and I guessed him to be part Cherokee or Choctaw—not Comanche; they're tall people. He had light brown unruly hair, blue eyes, a face that was something between square and round, and a stocky build overall. He was grimy, but in his case the grime made sense: A "shade-tree mechanic," he'd been working on a motorcycle engine when Lantana called him to the house. He'd hastily washed off the oil on his hands and had come on in, still in oily jeans and khaki shirt. He still hadn't said anything to me, and there wasn't much use in anybody saying anything until Lantana got tired of crying.

I hiccuped and thought, "Oh, no, am I going to start *that* again?" I hiccuped twice more and then burped embarrassingly, which was ridiculous; I hadn't even had a Coke with the burger I'd grabbed on the way over here. Even Lantana stopped crying for a second to stare at me with startled eyes.

"Lady, you okay?" Billy Jack asked.

"I'm fine," I tried to say, but unfortunately I hiccuped in the middle.

"You sure? Could I get you a glass of water? Or some iced tea? I've got some right here."

I accepted the glass of water gratefully; it helped a little, and the hiccups faded off and finally stopped.

Lantana lifted her head, blew her nose on a Kleenex she pitched in the general direction of the trash can, and asked, "Okay, you told me. Now why are you here?"

I took a deep breath. It seemed to me I was doing a little more than my fair share of breaking the news to people, and I was getting tired of it. "All this is probably going to be in the newspaper by tomorrow, what of it isn't already. I figured you ought to know about it ahead of time, and I needed to ask you a few questions."

"You honestly think my brother helped to kill that little girl?"

"It looks that way, Mrs. Turner."

Lantana chuckled drily. "Mrs. Turner? You been calling me Lantana ever since you's born, you might as well keep at it."

"Okay, Lantana. But—"

"What I was going to say, I just don't see how Patrick'd do that. He's no killer. Not Patrick."

"Lantana, he killed Sonny. We both know that."

"Yeah, but that was different. He killed Sonny because of that bitch Susie, allus wiggling her bottom at everything in pants, and Sonny, he wasn't immune to nobody wiggling her bottom at him. And I figure Susie, she must of wiggled real good, you know what I mean."

"I know what you mean."

"And Patrick, he was so blame mad and jealous he didn't think about Susie wiggling her bottom, he just thought about Sonny screwing around with her—you know, you done broke up my happy home? If Sonny'd of stayed hid out a couple more days Patrick'd have got over it and just sent Susie on about her business. He didn't go to kill Sonny only he was so blame mad he couldn't think. He was bawling like a baby two seconds after it happened."

That was true. I'd been there. I'd seen it.

"But Patrick wouldn't hurt a kid," she added. "He loved kids. Always did. If that bitch Susie would've given him kids instead of going around wiggling her bottom wouldn't none of that have ever happened."

"He might have changed, Lantana. People do."

"But Patrick, I saw him last—what was it, Billy Jack, about three weeks ago? He's still—he was still the same ol' Patrick. A-playing around with the young'uns."

"He might not have realized the other person intended to kill the child, though, Lantana. He might have thought—"

"You mean he might have thought they'd just get the money and give the kid back?"

"Yeah," I said, "that's a possibility, you know."

"Well, maybe," Lantana said. "But thing is, Patrick never was the kind of person to care much about money. I mean—I don't know how to make you understand. He liked things, sure, if they was his things. But he didn't never want nobody else's things, not even clear back when he was a little kid. He wasn't—" she stopped to ponder, and then used a very unexpected word. "He wasn't covetous."

One-forty, and I was back at the Federal Office Building. Cooper arrived two minutes early, which was somewhat better than I had expected; Goslin had indicated he had a reputation for unreliability, and that, coming from Goslin, suggested he was some more kind of unreliable.

He was, at a guess, twenty-six. His hair, an indeterminate shade between brown and blond, lay flat on his forehead. His chubby face had no real expression at all; his rounded contours seemed to sag. I wondered, briefly, what he'd look like when he grew up, whether his face would ever grow any individuality. Probably he'd never look a lot different from the way he looked as I watched him from the window, slamming the door of his pickup truck and trotting up the walk to the door the guard held open for him.

"Hi, Coop, thanks for coming in," Castillo said. He made his voice sound a lot friendlier than it ever did when he was talking normally.

"Yeah, well, one of those things," Cooper said meaninglessly. "Goslin said you needed to see me. I don't know what-all I can tell you; I mean, when Bassinger drove I wasn't there, o' course, and so I just met him a few times, and—"

"I realize that," Castillo said. "I just need you to help me work something out. This is Deb Ralston, with the Fort Worth Police Department. We're working together on this case." He couldn't manage to sound casual when he said that; his glance at me was eloquent.

"H'lo," Cooper said in my direction, and folded his

length into a chair with as little realization of his size as Hal now seems to have. And Hal, who at the age of sixteen has suddenly expanded from five-feet-ten to six-feet-three and is still growing, keeps running into walls that seem to step out in front of him.

"Thanks for coming in," I said, and Cooper shrugged and looked at Castillo.

"You got a good memory, right?" Castillo said. "Goslin says you do."

Goslin had said no such thing. But Cooper wouldn't know that.

"Yeah, well, I guess I do. Good's most people, anyways."

"Okay, think about your route."

"Yeah?" Cooper closed his eyes and cocked his head to the left and up. That, I assumed, meant he was thinking about his route. "What about it?"

"You turn onto Four Mile Road. What do you see?"

"First there's this yella' house on the left, belongs to somebody named Green. They've got a yappety little dog that runs after my truck—sometime I'm afraid I'm gonna hit the son of a bitch if they don't start keeping it off the road. Then there's a trailer house on the right. It's a sort of dirty blue and it hasn't been there long. They cleared out just enough brush to make room for it—no yard or anything—and strung power lines across the road from the Greens. They've got this girl about twelve—I see her on Saturdays, riding a boy's red bike—and a little boy I keep seeing outdoors just in a diaper no matter what the weather is. And how I know he's a boy is ever' now and then he's outdoors without the diaper."

Surprise, surprise. Cooper did have a good memory. Castillo told him so. "Now think about Box Two-twenty."

"It's on the left. There's nine boxes—" his voice trailed off. "Nine—" he sounded uncertain. Then he opened his eyes. "I'll be damned."

"You've remembered something?"

"Yeah! Last week there was ten boxes. There's only s'posed to be—that's weird. That is really weird. There was ten, but Friday it was back to nine. I'm used to people putting up boxes—somebody's moved in a trailer house down on the creek, or something like that—but taking them away, now that is really strange."

"You can swear to that?" Castillo leaned forward.

"You bet I can!" Cooper's voice was emphatic. "That tenth box, it was big enough you could use it for a doghouse for a cocker spaniel. I mean it was *big,* and it drooped over the edge of the post all antegoddlin, and—look, I'll tell you how bad it was put on. I had this package to deliver and as big as the box was the package fit right in, only soon as I closed the box up the damn box fell off the post. I had to get out of the truck and set it back on the post—well, I guess I didn't have to, but I did—and I stuck a note in there telling 'em they better get it fixed. But then Friday—Friday I didn't notice it wasn't there because I was so used to it not being there, you know what I mean, but now I think about it—"

"You ever deliver anything else to that box?"

"Uh-uh. Just that one package."

"How big was the package?"

"Oh, I don't know, hard to say. About like so." He was waving his hands around, framing the outline of a box.

"Compare it to something in this office." Quite deliberately Castillo had set a Tony Lama boot box on a shelf beside his books, along with two or three other boxes of assorted sizes.

As neither of us would have dared to hope before this

conversation, Cooper homed in on the boot box. "That," he said definitely. "Just about that size. As best as I can remember it was just about exactly that size."

"Okay, what did it look like?"

"Look like? Oh, it was wrapped with brown paper and taped shut and it had the address wrote on it in black."

"Any name?"

"Uh-uh. Just the address."

"You see anybody pick it up?" I held my breath, waiting for an answer to that question. But I should have been able to guess—we both should have been able to guess—what the answer would be.

"No, it was still sitting there when I left."

"Okay. You've been a lot of help. Tomorrow when you get in off your route I want you to come in and sign a statement."

"Yeah? Don't I got to make a statement before I can sign it?"

"You've just made it," I told him, indicating the tape recorder running on the desk.

"Yeah?" Cooper said. "But all I did was tell you—"

"Cooper, what the hell do you think a statement is?" Castillo demanded.

Cooper shrugged. "Mister, I ain't been to no law school."

"You've got some more kind of a good visual memory, though," I said.

His reply was totally unexpected. "I damn well better have. I'm an artist."

"An artist?" I repeated. "Then why are you working in a post office?"

Cooper stood up and grinned wryly. "Lady, you ever try to make a living working as an artist?" And as he turned to go the light caught him at a different angle and I could see small lines and creases around his eyes and mouth I hadn't seen before.

I didn't have to go on wondering what he'd be like when he grew up. He was grown up now.

"He wasn't covetous?" Harry repeated, eyebrows raised. "That's a funny thing to say."

"Not really," I said. "Lantana was raised in the Baptist Church; all the Kellys were, and she'd probably have memorized the Ten Commandments when she was in the fifth grade or thereabouts."

"They went; that doesn't mean they listened."

"You're cynical. Lantana listened; I know she did. She's a good woman. She's ignorant and she's poor and she's probably a little bit stupid, but she does the best she can. Patrick—maybe not. Maybe he didn't listen. But he'd have known the words whether he heard them or not."

"Maybe," Harry said, "but when you come to think of it, not very many people even know what *covetousness* means. I'm not quite sure I do myself." He stopped and regarded me solemnly. "You sure you feel like cooking, Deb? You look awful."

"Gee, thanks."

"You know what I mean. We can go out, if you'd rather."

"I wouldn't rather. I feel more like cooking supper than I do like putting my shoes on again."

About two seconds later I felt like screaming. Harry, since buying the ham radio about a year ago, has gone radio-happy. There is now a CB radio in the bedroom so he can listen to truckers and channel nine emergencies until he goes to sleep or until I throw a tantrum and demand the radio be turned off at once, whichever comes first. The newest acquisition is a police and fire scanner in the kitchen, where we can listen to it while we eat. Harry turned it on. I turned it down. "I'm trying to *think*," I protested.

Harry seated himself expectantly at the table. "So think already."

I handed him a stack of plates. "You could set the table while I think." I returned to stirring the spaghetti sauce I'd started well before he offered to take us out, and brooded.

"You want to think out loud?" Harry asked after a few minutes of silence.

"Oh, I don't know." I turned distractedly, to drain the spaghetti into a colander in the sink. "It's just, if she's right that Patrick wasn't covetous—I know as well as I know my own name that he was mixed up in that kidnapping. They used his mailing address for the ransom; the child was put in his pantry. It just doesn't make sense. If he wasn't covetous why would he do it?"

"Maybe he was forced into it?"

"I don't think he was, though. I just keep thinking—suppose, for some reason, he thought French had shafted him? Suppose he thought for some reason French owed him?"

"Why would he think that?"

"I don't know. Maybe French sold him a car and somebody got killed in it—only I don't know who would have, because if he ever married again Lantana didn't tell me, and she specifically said he didn't have any children. But I just keep thinking—okay, from the autopsy, the child wasn't deliberately harmed. She was shut up in a car trunk, that's all. They probably didn't know she had asthma, they didn't know shutting her up in a car trunk was going to kill her. So suppose he thought French owed him? Suppose he thought French owed him and that was the only way he had of getting whatever he thought French owed him?"

"Well, what was the connection, then?"

"I don't know. French said he never knew a Patrick Kelly."

"French doesn't have to have known Patrick Kelly for Kelly to think French owes him." I turned and began stirring the spaghetti sauce, and Harry, apparently sensing I was through talking, turned up the little Bearcat scanner. As it came into my hearing range it was saying, "I checked with the sergeant and he says if there's no stolen just have it towed."

"Have it towed where?" Danny Shea's voice demanded.

"To the pound, Shea, where do we always tow abandoned cars?" Greg Vinson's voice sounded annoyed, as people's voices usually do when they have to deal with Danny Shea.

I turned the radio off again.

"Why did you do that?" Harry asked. "I like to know what's going on."

"So do I," I told him, "but not during dinner. I'll be back in a minute; I'm going to go call the hospital to see how Livingston's doing. Would you kind of watch the spaghetti sauce and make sure it doesn't burn?"

"I will be glad to watch the spaghetti sauce," Harry said. "Now you're getting smart."

"Uh-huh, smart aleck." I headed for the telephone. But I knew what Harry was talking about. Every now and then, when I'm brooding over a case, I manage to let supper burn to a crisp. Harry usually accuses me of doing it deliberately. If he was the one who had to scrub the pans he would be quite aware I would never do it deliberately.

The hospital said Bill Livingston was conscious but had no memory of anything more recent than three days ago. The hospital also said they would appreciate it if fewer police officers would call the hospital every five minutes, and although they understood that I had a legitimate need to know, surely I could understand—

I told them I could understand. I went back to the kitchen and resumed stirring the spaghetti sauce, which Harry was watching intently but not stirring.

"What was that all about on the radio anyway?" he asked me.

"On the radio when?"

"Just before you turned it off. Sounded like somebody must have been asking stupid questions."

"Oh, that was Shea. He always asks stupid questions. This time he couldn't figure out what to do with an abandoned car. And the policy about abandoned cars hasn't changed in the last fifteen years to my knowledge. Maybe longer."

"Oh?"

"Yeah. You run 'em for stolen and if there's no stolen you try to contact the owner and if you can't contact the owner you have the car towed to the pound. After it's been around long enough that you're sure it's abandoned, that is—that means you sticker it and watch the sticker, or else if it's blocking a driveway or something you go on and have it towed right away. I mean you just don't tow it because it's been left overnight in front of a supermarket with a dead battery."

"Yeah?" Harry drawled. "How does a supermarket get a dead battery?"

I guess he was getting even with me for causing him to land his plane in a bad place. Why else would he ask a question like that?

· 5 ·

"THIS IS MONDAY," I protested sleepily. "I'm scheduled off on Monday." I'd gone back to bed after getting Harry and Hal off, and the phone had been an unceremonious awakening.

"So, you were scheduled off on Sunday, too," Captain Millner replied. "Come on in, Deb."

"When am I supposed to *breathe*?"

"You asked for it."

That wasn't exactly true. I'd asked to be on the homicide squad, not the major case squad, but a token woman is likely to get put wherever she is most noticeable. The fact that I had turned out to be somewhat more than a token was now immaterial.

But even detectives were allowed days off, I grumbled to myself as I dressed. I'd planned to do laundry this afternoon.

But maybe I'd be lucky. Maybe they'd just need me

for an hour or two. Maybe I'd still have time to do laundry.

"What is it?" I demanded in Captain Millner's office forty-five minutes later, deliberately keeping my voice just on the near side of sulky.

Captain Millner, several report forms in his hand, didn't look up. "You take a report from a Deborah Mossberg Saturday?" Now he did look up. "Or rather, *refuse* to take a report?"

I sat down. "Yeah. It was a domestic dispute. We really didn't have any business in it at all, and if anybody but Danny Shea had taken the initial report detectives'd have never been called on it at all." But I could feel a cold hard knot forming in my stomach. What if—

I didn't let myself think any more what if's.

"What did you tell the mother?"

"The situation was, the father had visitation rights and she—"

"What did you tell the mother?" Millner interrupted.

"Look, you have to understand—"

"The background. I know. I always have to understand the background. But right now I don't give a damn about the background. I just want to know what you told the mother."

I took a deep breath. "I told her if the child wasn't back by Monday to give us a call then. Did she call up and complain?"

"No. She just gave us another call." Millner tossed the printout of Shea's report across the desk to me. "You better get on out there. She specifically asked for you, so she wouldn't have to explain everything twice."

I didn't say, "Oh, shit." But I admit I thought it.

Deborah Mossberg didn't have her makeup on this time. She was pale, and without mascara and eyeliner her eyes and eyebrows were almost invisible; this gave her a curiously childlike look. Her hand shook slightly, almost imperceptibly, as she lit a cigarette with a hand yellowed by smoke. "You said if she wasn't back Monday—"

"Yes." I felt a little more sympathetic this time, but only a little. "Have you heard anything at all from your ex-husband?"

"Uh-uh. I mean I called that service station and they said he hadn't been in."

At least now she was making a little effort herself. That was good. "Could I see a picture of her?"

Candy didn't look malnourished. That was my first thought—Candy didn't look malnourished. She was, in fact, a pretty child, with black hair and blue eyes. Very curly black hair, to judge from the picture; she was like a brunette Little Orphan Annie. She was, in the picture, wearing a pink sweatshirt with a white heart on it. On the white heart was a pink cat with very long whiskers and jeweled eyes.

"I buy her pretty clothes," Deborah said. "If—if I didn't work so many hours I couldn't buy her such pretty clothes. But I just keep thinking—I just keep thinking."

I didn't ask the direction of her thoughts. Maybe, I thought, maybe if Rick kept his daughter away long enough I wouldn't have to call welfare after all. "Let me get some information from you. Name—is it really Candy, or—"

"It's really Candace. But I call her Candy. Rick doesn't; he says it sounds silly. He calls her Candace. I don't think it sounds silly to call her Candy, do you?" Her childlike air was even more noticeable; it seemed she was appealing to me for permission to continue using her child's nickname.

"It sounds okay to me," I assured her. "Lots of little girls are called Candy."

"Well, I thought so too," she said.

"Candace Mossberg—" I was writing. "Does she have a middle name?"

"Jean. That was my mother's name, Jean. I thought it would be nice to name her after my mother. But my mother wasn't named Candace. I had a friend named that. They called her Candy, but she had taffy-colored hair. I thought Candy was going to—she had this real light color of hair when she was born, but then when she was about two it got darker."

"Lots of kids do that. Candace Jean, all right." Her date of birth. She was six in October. Her height. Deborah didn't know her weight but said she was in size 6X clothes. Was there a picture I could have? Deborah gave me a picture. Her likes and dislikes?

"I don't know of anything she doesn't like," Deborah said vaguely. "She likes dogs and cats and other kids and chocolate and clothes. She doesn't like oatmeal much but then neither do I. Rick does. I don't know why. I can't think why anybody would really like oatmeal but then on the other hand I can't think why anybody would pretend to if they didn't. Unless they thought eating oatmeal was one of those things all proper people do."

"I don't like oatmeal either," I agreed. "It kind of sticks in the back of my throat."

"Yeah, like that," Deborah agreed eagerly.

"Okay, do you have any idea what she would have been wearing when she went missing?"

"Yeah, I checked her clothes. A pair of jeans—Gitano

brand—and a blue sweater. Pullover, I mean, not cardigan."

"What shade of blue?"

"Oh, powder blue. I don't like that royal blue for little girls, do you?"

"One of my daughters could wear it and one couldn't," I replied. And yes, we were far afield from what we should be talking about, but on the other hand Deborah was settling down visibly and the information we really needed was flowing more freely now.

"What age are your daughters?"

I had to stop and think before I could answer, "Twenty-three and twenty."

"Gee, and another one coming now? That's the shits," Deborah said sympathetically. "Just when you thought you were all through, I guess?"

"Oh, well, I'm kind of looking forward to it," I said, not wanting to go into any detailed explanation now. "Let me get some information from you about Rick, now," I added.

"Rick. Okay, you want a picture of him?"

"That would help, yes, especially if it's current."

The picture was probably a year old, Deborah decided after considerable dithering; it was taken right before she decided to file for divorce.

Rick was lean; his hair was sandy blond and his eyes were blue. He was, in the picture, tossing Candy in the air, and Candy was laughing gleefully. Height? Oh, well, she guessed he was about five-ten, and how was she supposed to know what he weighed? A hundred and thirty-five maybe, did that sound right?

I told her that sounded right, if he was five-ten and lean.

Rick's name was Richard Dwayne Mossberg and he

was twenty-eight and he stayed in the army a while—Candy was born in an army hospital. He really liked the army and he got to be a sergeant and he wanted to stay in but Deborah didn't like moving around that much so Rick got out of the army only he stayed in the reserves and he was always going to drills and stuff—well, not always, one weekend a month, but still—and he got a job with an oil drilling company and then he got laid off and he couldn't get another job and he wanted to go back in the army only Deborah didn't want to, they wanted to send him to Germany of all places and he wanted her to go along and what was she supposed to do in Germany when she didn't even speak German, and so he didn't get a job except that little stupid job at the service station and one time he sold magazines over the telephone only nobody bought them so he didn't make any money and so Deborah was supporting the family and so she got good and fed up with it and so she got a divorce.

She was out of breath by the time she stopped talking.

I would have gone with Harry, if the Marines had sent him places I could go, I thought. Only they didn't. I thought, briefly, of some of the places he had been, while I sat home in Fort Worth and never missed a newscast.

But my problems didn't have anything to do with the missing child. "How well do Rick and Candy get along?"

"Real good," Deborah said.

"Rick never mistreats her or anything?"

"He wouldn't do anything like that."

I got Rick's address and the name and address of the service station where he worked. "What relatives does Rick have in the area?"

His mother lived in Hurst. She was mad at Rick for not having a job and mad at Deborah for working in a bar even if that *was* the only way to get the bills paid and she said Deborah was neglecting Candy but when Deborah asked her if she wanted to baby-sit she said that was taking advantage of her good nature but when Deborah got a different baby-sitter she said that showed Deborah didn't trust her own mother-in-law.

She was out of breath again, and by now I was beginning to have a small amount of sympathy for Deborah as well as for Rick. I got that address too—I might or might not need it—and then asked, "Do you think Rick would have taken her anywhere? If he did, where might he go?"

"He didn't have anywhere to go," Deborah said. "Look, you don't understand. He doesn't have any money. The only place he's got to go is to Dallas to look for work, but he doesn't know anybody there and he wanted us to just sleep in the truck until he found a job and got a paycheck, and look, you can't live in a truck for a month or so with a baby, I mean a six-year-old, now can you? And don't tell me people do it because I know people do it but that doesn't mean I want to. But he sure wouldn't try that alone with Candy without me to look after her; what would he do, leave her sitting in the truck all day while he was at work? The only other thing he could do is try to go back in the army and he could do that by himself but he sure couldn't take Candy with him."

And that was perfectly true.

"I'll see what I can find out," I told her. "But you need to know that I'm tied up on another case right now, so some other police will probably want to come talk with you. I'll be sure they know everything you've told me, okay? When you get a different officer it doesn't mean the police aren't trying; it just means—"

"Just find Candy," Deborah interrupted.

"Let me have the phone number where you work."

"You think I'm going to *work*?"

I wasn't supposed to be at work. But since I was there I figured I might as well stay. So I went to my desk and pawed through my in-basket, disposing of as much as I could as fast as I could so that it wouldn't overflow onto my desk as it has been known to do when I was busy with other things.

While I was doing that Otto Castillo came in and, without so much as a by-your-leave, sat down at Dutch Van Flagg's desk, directly across from me, to make a long-distance telephone call. On *our* phone. When he's got a perfectly good WATS line or something like that of his own that is being paid for out of *our* tax dollars.

But it turned out he wanted me to pick up the extension and listen in while he talked with a Dallas detective, a fellow named Beckman, who was heading up the kidnap task force over there. Beckman said a Dallas detective was on her way over to meet with the Fort Worth people. "Her name's Aline Brinkley. She had to go pick up some stuff first, but I figure she ought to be there around noon. So you can wait and ask her—"

"Okay, well, the Fort Worth detective is on the line here. Deb Ralston."

"Deb Ralston?"

"Yeah. Major case squad. She's—uh—in charge of the city's end of the case."

"Oh hell," Beckman said, "I sent Aline 'cause I figured it'd be a man handling it out there and I wanted to make sure we'd get a female slant on the investigation. Now what—"

"Don't worry," I told him, "we've got plenty of men in Fort Worth. Including Otto." Who grimaced at me before speaking.

"Look, Beckman," Otto said, "I'm not sure whether Brinkley would know what I'm asking about. I'm not sure anybody knows."

"Try asking."

"I'm guessing it's probably going to be a negative anyway."

"Try asking," Beckman repeated, not very patiently.

"Did anybody find Helen's purse?"

"Man, we're talking about an eight-year-old. They don't start carrying purses that young."

"Helen did." He detailed, and Beckman whistled. "So what I'm thinking is, if you don't have it and we don't have it, then it just might be in the car she was transported in. And I should have asked French what it looked like but he had left before I thought of it."

"Well, it could be in the car," Beckman said, "but you're forgetting one thing."

"Which is?"

"This is Dallas. How long do you think a purse—even a kid's purse—is going to lay on the sidewalk or in the street? And remember how long it was before French reported it? It don't mean shit that we didn't find it."

"Yeah, I know, somebody could have stolen it, but it's worth going on, at least as a possibility. So you didn't find it?"

"We didn't find it. We didn't know to look for one."

"French absolutely, positively, did not tell you she had one? Or Mrs. French either?"

"I don't want to lie to you. Hold on and let me check on the statements." That took a few minutes; then

Beckman was back on the line. "Absolutely no word. Nobody told us to look for a purse. That's firm."

"She was kidnapped from the front of the school— what did the school think when she went missing? What time of day was the snatch anyway?"

"About one o'clock. She'd gone home for lunch—she did that a lot. It wasn't normal practice at the school but her house was real close by and she had a lot of allergies, so it just seemed easier. It was a pretty day and she begged to walk back to school. Her mother normally drove her, but she was kind of busy and so she let her walk. When she didn't show back up, the teacher— a Sister Mary Margaret—just assumed she'd had another asthma attack and didn't think any more about it. Especially when the parents called the next day and just said Helen wouldn't be in for a while."

"Okay, what's the chance the purse wound up in lost and found at the school? Maybe some kid found it in front of the school and turned it in?"

"I'll check on it. You know what it looked like? Oh, no, you said you didn't. Okay, I'll call Mrs. French and get it from her. You going to be in your office?"

"Uh-uh. I'm over at the Fort Worth PD. Major case squad. I'll be here a few more minutes anyway."

"I'll call you back."

By now there were postal inspectors busy all over Fort Worth. I knew a lot of what they were doing, and whatever they were doing was something—some things—I wouldn't have to duplicate. They were methodically looking up everybody Patrick Kelly had ever known, because by now a medical examiner and a crime laboratory had said there was a good chance that Patrick Kelly and Roy Bassinger were killed by the same gun. That wasn't a certainty, of course, because it is never possible to say what weapon a load of shot comes out of. But the lab had agreed with Habib that the shot in each killing came from a very old shell, and while it wasn't completely impossible that two different small-caliber shotguns loaded with very old shells would be involved in these certainly interrelated crimes, it certainly wasn't what anybody would want to call probable.

Somebody killed Roy Bassinger because he was in the wrong place at the wrong time, and nobody would learn anything by investigating Roy Bassinger's past. But most likely—in fact almost certainly—Patrick Kelly was killed for personal reasons. Which meant he was killed by somebody who knew him. Which meant somebody, somewhere, was going to have some idea who had known Patrick Kelly well enough to kill him.

Otto decided to go see what his crew of postal inspectors was doing, and I took the time to escape this case a few minutes and go see what I could find out about Rick Mossberg. I'd have to hand the case over to somebody else soon, of course, but if I could clear it up fast—

I was feeling bad, now, about not having taken the report Saturday, although no police officer with any sense at all would have taken that report.

And I did know where Haley's Mobil Station was.

"I haven't seen Rick since Friday," Rex Haley told me. He'd owned Haley's for thirty years; his wrinkled, leathery face and indelibly oil-stained work clothes told of survival rather than success, and a rusted Flying Red Horse logo still hung over the door. "I cain't afford to pay him much—the missus and me, we pretty well run the place by ourselves—but look, Rick's allus been a good boy, and a man's got to have some self-respect. I let him pump gas when I go home for supper. And I let him live in that old trailer out by my farm pond—I put it out there fifteen years ago, so's I could spend the night out there when I wanted to get up early to go fishing, but I don't do much fishing anymore noway, and he's got to have somewheres to live other than with that bitch of a mother of his. I told him he could pay for the use of the trailer and utilities by plowing my fire-lines and checking them to be sure they stay clear. It's a job that's got to get done, and I sure don't have time to do it myself. And I pay him twenty dollars a week for watching the station while I'm at supper. He does odd jobs, lawn work and stuff like that, for a couple of doctors and lawyers—doesn't make much, but it keeps him fed. Lucky he has the pickup clear, because if he didn't he'd sure as hell lose it. There ain't no way he could keep up payments. He keeps the insurance paid on it—that's state law, acourse—but he doesn't have nothing but liability. Cain't afford nothing else. I don't know what he'll do if he ever has a wreck. You damn sure cain't get around worth a damn without no car."

"That's for sure," I agreed, "but about Friday—"

"Just, the school called to see if he was here—he wasn't scheduled to come in till five, but he comes in early a lot of the time. I cain't pay him for it. But he says it's a heap better than just setting around on his ass—behind, excuse me, ma'am."

"That's okay. So the school called him. About what time was that?"

"About one-thirty, two, thereabouts. He tole me his little girl was sick and he had to go get her. So he went to get her and he brought her back by here—she's a cute little thaing, and he wanted to get her a Coke out of the machine, figuring it'd settle her stomach, only

· 98 ·

she upchucked it as soon as she drank it. Well, you could see she was really feeling puny, and he said he guessed he'd better take her out to the trailer 'cause her mama was at work. Then he left and I called Margie and told her I wasn't getting in for supper and she better plan to bring it over here." He gestured at his house, which was directly behind the gasoline station.

"Where is the trailer located?"

"I told you, ma'am, it's out on my farm."

"I understand that," I said, "but where is the farm located?"

"Oh, well, it's kind of off Old Denton Road. I keep six head of cattle out there, but I don't get out there much myself anymore. Rick, he feeds 'em when they need hay, and checks their salt blocks, but mostly they feed theirselves. I got a good pasture."

I got exact directions to the trailer and drove out there, feeling guilty, because it was a long way out of the city, which made it a long way out of my jurisdiction. And I was supposed to be on a different case.

But Helen French was dead. There wasn't anything—much—I could do to help her, at least not directly.

But Candy Mossberg was—I hoped—alive. And I'd like her to stay that way.

The trailer was there. But there wasn't any pickup truck parked near it, no little girl playing outside, and the door I tried cautiously—and illegally—was locked.

"And that's how it is," I told Millner. "I don't know where she'd have gone—I don't know where he'd have taken her. From what the mother says it sounds just about impossible for him to have taken her anywhere. I did spot a few leads to follow up, but I don't think they're going to get us anywhere. You don't want me to stay on this, do you? I don't see how I can handle it and the Helen French thing both at once, but I feel so bad about—"

"I'd have done the same thing," Millner interrupted. "Saturday it was a domestic dispute we had no legal right to get involved in. Now it may have grown into something more, but that's not a hundred percent certain yet. No, you can't work everything at once any more than anybody else can. Dictate your report and then turn it over to Dutch."

"Dutch? I thought he was on—"

"He's through with it, all except finishing up reports. He's got Maynard in the county jail as of nine-fifteen this morning. Turn it over to Dutch. Oh, but you can go ahead and get a lookout on the truck—I don't know how long it would take Dutch to get around to it."

If Dutch was still making reports on the Maynard case, which had been an extremely interesting fraud that had lost several elderly people their homes, he'd be tied up quite a while longer. So Millner still didn't think Candy Mossberg was really going to be missing.

I hoped he was right.

I sat down at the desk and my telephone rang. It was Beckman, hunting Otto Castillo. I hadn't the least idea where Castillo was and told him so, but I'd be glad to know about the purse myself.

"A kangaroo bag—okay." That's a canvas bag with a little change purse attached with a strap. "Red, okay. What would it have had in it besides the inhaler?"

It would have contained money, about two dollars in change, a door key, some pictures, a library card with no name on it, only a number strip. The only thing with her name on it was the prescription inhaler. The purse wasn't at her home, and it wasn't at the lost and found at school. It might have been stolen from in front of the school, but then again it might not have been.

It wasn't with her body at the house.

It might be in the car where she'd been transported. But then again it might not be.

It was a possibility. That's all. Police work has to move in a series of possibilities.

Possibilities . . . I had a friend who might possibly be able to help.

The FBI has worked out a personality study thing. The way it works is, at least theoretically it is possible to tell quite a lot about a person's personality and background by the way a crime is committed. Some of their agents are trained in this technique; they run schools to train local police officers in it.

Not local schools. Schools at their national academy.

We had a few people who were theoretically trained in it. And of course, if we wanted to, we could always ask the Bureau for help.

I didn't want to ask the Bureau. Not when one of my closest friends is one of the finest psychiatrists in Texas.

I called Susan Braun and asked if she could possibly break away and meet me for lunch. She said she was sort of busy and I said it was sort of urgent.

She said she didn't have time to go anywhere but if I wanted to come out to Braun Clinic she could arrange for an extra tuna fish sandwich, about eleven.

A tuna fish sandwich sounded like exactly what I wanted.

Over the tuna fish sandwiches, I described the case to Susan. All right, both cases, because although I had been officially removed from the Mossberg case I still wasn't easy in my mind—well, conscience, anyway—over it.

That was the one Susan decided to address first. "I'm getting all this third hand, you know."

"Third hand?"

"Third hand. The father would be first hand. The mother would be second hand. You're third hand. So I don't have as much to go on as I'd like to get. But—she says he isn't violent?"

"She says she's never known him to be."

"But it was a bitter divorce?"

"Well, sort of, but he hasn't got any money—"

"That doesn't necessarily mean anything. If he thinks the child is being neglected—and from what you say he'd be right to think that—then it's possible he's decided to take the child and hightail it to Oklahoma or Arkansas and hope to hide out there. But if he wants his wife back too—"

"I think he does," I said. "She didn't say so, not exactly, but—"

"You're good at picking up the nuances. Yes. Well, my own guess is he's decided to give the mother a good scare, and he'll have the girl back in a few days."

"But she's missing school—wouldn't he care if—"

Susan shrugged. "Not necessarily. He might not even have thought of that. Just keep the lookout on the truck, that's the only suggestion I've got. But this other case—" She shook her head. "I don't know. I don't know how the FBI does that. You've got so little to go on. Of course it's obvious he knows French whether French knows him or not—"

"It is?" It wasn't all that obvious to me.

"Deb, I've never heard of a crook so stupid he'd expect a ransom to be *mailed* to him. He'd have sense

• 102 •

enough—if he had sense enough to stake out the school and watch for a day the little girl was walking, and be able to recognize her and pick her out from two hundred other little girls dressed the same—he'd have sense enough to know if a ransom is mailed the person who collects it'll be picked up at the other end. Which means he knew French well enough he knew French wouldn't call the police.

"Oh. Well, yeah, that makes sense."

Susan stopped to eat a potato chip. She ate another one, thoughtfully, and then looked out the window of her office, onto the grounds of her mental hospital, where several of her patients were planting a fall garden. "It keeps them busy and keeps their minds off their troubles," she'd told me when I asked why she'd added a large garden to the complex that already included a jogging track, riding stables, indoor swimming pools, and basketball and volleyball courts.

She has her own theories on how to cure mental illness. They don't always jibe with other people's theories, but they seem to work. At least as well as other people's theories do.

"What I *don't* understand," she said, half to herself, and stopped without telling me what she didn't understand. Turning back to face me, she asked, "Could the child have been hauled in the back of that car that was burning when you got there?"

"She could've been. If she was, her purse wasn't in it. Or her missing shoe. We did collect samples of the dust and stuff for the lab to look at, but they said something about a pink blanket and there wasn't a blanket back there either."

"So she might have had a pink blanket on her bed. All they can tell is that her clothing came in contact with a pink blanket at some time; they can't say for sure the pink blanket was in the trunk, can they?"

"They said they could. And labs can do a lot." There was a case in Australia I'd heard about where crime labs, doing an incredible amount of work, managed through pollen and leaf comparisons to trace a kidnap victim back not only to the neighborhood where he had been killed but even to the exact house, which had a rare imported tree in its yard, to get a conviction on a nasty kidnap-murder. "I don't know, maybe there was some oil on the blanket or something. They said the blanket was in the car and they seemed pretty sure about that."

"Okay." Susan fiddled with her fork, for no reason at all so far as I could see; her plate was now empty. "Kelly didn't start out to be a scapegoat. He was in on the planning; I don't know how far in on it, but unless the other man has a law enforcement background Kelly was in on the planning."

"What makes you say that?"

"You go think about it a while and you'll see it just as clear as I do."

"But if Kelly didn't start out to be a scapegoat how did they plan to disassociate him from—?"

"You check. I'll bet you anything you want to bet that Kelly wasn't getting his own mail there. He had a post office box in town. They didn't mean the child to die; that was an accident. You said even the ME said that. If she hadn't died she probably wouldn't have been taken to the farm at all. And she'd have been returned later and all Kelly would have had to do was say, 'I don't know anything about it; somebody must've put up a box there,' and could you have proved otherwise?"

"Yeah, probably."

"Probably. But you aren't sure. No. Kelly didn't think all of it up but he was in on the planning. Somebody who knew at least a little bit about how law enforcement officers work was in on the planning. But there was somebody else—somebody with a sneaky, devious mind—" Her voice trailed off. "I want to think about this a while," she said. "I've got some ideas but I want to think about this a while."

I left her to think about it. If Aline Brinkley was due in Fort Worth about noon I ought to be in my office to meet her. And that would take some hurrying, because it was a quarter of twelve already.

· 6 ·

She came into our office with her badge case open, a big blond woman, walking as if she had a quarrel with the universe. She was at least five-eleven, more like six feet, and though she wasn't fat now she'd run to fat if she ever quit exercising. Ignoring me—I was sorting through my in-basket, which had unaccountably filled back up while I was at lunch—she headed straight for the one man in the room. "I'm Detective Brinkley with the Dallas Police Department," she said loudly, her crisp voice sounding more northeastern than southern. "I'm looking for the man in charge of the French investigation."

"Oh, you are," Captain Millner drawled as I looked up quickly. "And just why would you be doing that?"

"We need to set up a coordination effort."

"And what, pray tell, is a coordination effort?"

Even more loudly—I was surprised the windows

weren't cracking—she said, "It has reference to the pooling of our—"

"Detective Brinkley. Ms. Brinkley. I know what it means to coordinate our efforts. But I never heard of a coordination effort. Suppose you have a talk with Detective Ralston."

Detective Brinkley, as I said, is around six feet tall. But Captain Millner is six feet two, and he looks more like a television policeman than anybody else I've ever seen. Anybody else would have backed down, after hearing the tone of his voice.

But Aline Brinkley wasn't anybody else. More loudly yet—did she think we were all hard of hearing in this hick town of over 400,000 people?—she demanded, "And just where do I *find*—"

This, I decided, had gone quite far enough. "I'm Deb Ralston."

"Oh." Detective Brinkley at least had the grace to look a little sheepish. "I'm Aline Brinkley. I thought you were the secretary."

"Even if I were the secretary you could have spoken to me; I was the one closest to the door and you came right in past me as if I had suddenly turned invisible. What are you, one of those people who thinks she's more equal than anybody else?"

Aline Brinkley was a full head taller than me, but then I am well used to backing down people who are taller than I am. Looking even more sheepish, Aline said, "I think I got up too early this morning."

"Poor you. Counting today I've worked seven days straight, overtime on three of them. I *think* my next day off is five days away. We're well into the twentieth century in Tarrant County, Brinkley. Now do we work together like civilized people, which means we are po-

lite to the secretaries as well as to the sworn officers, or
do you want to get back in your kiddie car and pedal it
right back to Dallas?"

"Can we start over?"

"If you want to try."

Surprisingly, Aline Brinkley marched out into the hall
and meandered back into the major case squadroom.
"I'm Aline Brinkley," she announced, with a small grin
hovering around her mouth. "I'm a detective with the
Dallas Police Department. Could you tell me where I
can find the officer in charge of this end of the French
case?"

"That's me," I said, not smiling at all. "I'm Deb
Ralston, and this is my supervisor, Captain Millner."

Captain Millner was grinning openly as he acknowl-
edged the introduction.

Aline Brinkley, it seemed, was now ready to be
friendly. I wasn't. Not yet.

Not until we were out on the road, in the detective
car assigned to me, and Aline said, "Sorry."

"For what?"

"For when I came in. I mean, you'd think everybody
would be used to policewomen by now and that nobody
would have to carry on like that. But I've been treated
like dog shit so many times that now everywhere I go I
try to go in like I own the place, and back down and act
human later. I guess you must have even more trouble
than I do, huh?"

"Well," I said, "when you're my size you can't play
like the white tornado. So I just go in and explain who I
am and what I'm doing there. So what if they don't like
women being cops? They don't have to. Otto doesn't.
But he has to work with me just the same."

"Who's Otto?"

So I explained who Otto was, and by the time I got through with that explanation we were at the Kelly farmhouse.

Which, of course, we should have searched Sunday, and would have, except that recent court decisions have decided you now need a search warrant to search a crime scene without the consent of the owner. We'd stretched the law enough to remove the bodies, but beyond that we'd decided the house wasn't going anywhere, and it's easier to get search warrants on Monday.

We'd done a cursory walk-through to be sure there were no more victims—that much surely ought to be legal—but beyond that we'd just stationed an armed guard on the front porch.

The fact that our first armed guard had been knocked in the head had probably compromised our crime scene. But there wasn't anything we could do about that now. And we did finally have the search warrant.

Carlos Amado was sitting on the front porch in blue jeans, shotgun across his lap and radio on the floor beside him, scratching the dog's ears. The dog, looking as smug as only a feist can, did not move; he only looked up at me, flapped his tail halfheartedly on the steps a couple of times, and glanced at Aline curiously. He didn't even bother to bark, to announce her as a stranger, before he turned adoringly back to Carlos.

If he'd been my dog he would be loudly threatening to eat Aline for lunch. But then my dog is half pit bull. "Dog, you're a sycophant," I said.

"I fed him coffee," Carlos said.

"You did what?" asked Aline. The carefully controlled expression on her face, when I introduced Carlos, told me she spoke Spanish: His name means Charles Lover, and he hates it.

"Feists like coffee. I fed him coffee. Actually, what happened was, I set the cup down on the floor and he helped himself and I didn't think I wanted it back after that. Are you taking over here? Am I allowed to leave?" He produced a histrionic sigh. Members of the intelligence and stakeout squads are picked for a number of things including, I sometimes think, their acting ability.

"No, don't take off, Carlos," I said, "we'll just be here long enough to search, and I don't know yet when we can release the house."

"Well, look, you mind if I go ten-seven for a while, anyway? I've been out here since seven and I'm just about to starve. I was supposed to be doing something else today and I didn't know to bring a lunch."

"Go ahead," I said. "I don't think we're likely to have any interference out here, and we'll be a couple of hours anyway."

"Thanks. I'll leave you the dog," he offered.

"Take the dog if you want to," I said. "That's not a real dog anyway. Real dogs bark."

"The dog did nothing in the nighttime or the daytime either," Carlos said. "Come on, pooch, let's go get a hamburger."

I walked on past him, through the door, Aline right behind me. Living room. Dining room. Kitchen. Had it really been almost two days ago that I was last here? The smell was the same; the flies still buzzed.

A downstairs parlor that must once, ninety years ago, have been the ladies' retiring room—the Kellys had money, I'd been told, once, though they lost it a long time before the Depression.

Upstairs, four bedrooms and a very small bathroom

sitting on what must once have been an upstairs veran-
dah. Above that, an attic reached by a narrow staircase
in the back corner of a back bedroom—unfortunately, a
very full attic. And below the kitchen, a root cellar
reached by a narrow staircase in the screened-in back
porch, its pull-up door almost hidden by a rusted-out
wringer washer.

I may have been overly optimistic in telling Carlos
we'd be through searching in two hours.

There wasn't much furniture left. Except for the living room, what little there was was in tatters, and it
appeared that most of the house hadn't been cleaned in
years. Dust lay thick and heavy on most floors, in places
covering dead beetles so thoroughly only their shapes
were discernible. There weren't many cockroaches,
probably because there hadn't been anything much for
them to feed on, but almost certainly there were spiders.

I do not like spiders.

And there were footprints all over the house, tracked
through the heavy layers of dust. Maybe Saturday, if
anyone had been thinking, it would have been possible
to distinguish between the prints of police and sus-
pects. Today it wasn't. Too many people had tramped
through the house, and one more walk-through wasn't
going to matter.

That walk-through complete, we started to search.

Methodical. Start at the bottom and work up. We
couldn't separate and search two areas at once, because
there has to be somebody to verify any find.

Fortunately Beckman's telephone call from Dallas
had come before we'd finished the paperwork on the
search warrant. So our list of specific things sought included a red kangaroo purse, a door key, a prescription

inhaler, photographs and library card and two dollars in change, all the property of Helen French, deceased. The cash mailed by her father, two hundred fifty thousand dollars in small bills, serial numbers unknown. A Tony Lama boot box. Wrapping paper addressed to Box 220-J, on a rural route in Fort Worth, Texas.

The rule is this: You may look anywhere the things listed on your warrant might be found, and any other contraband you find in those places may be seized. But if you look a place nothing in your warrant could possibly fit and find contraband, that's tough. You leave it right where it is. Thus you don't look in a dresser drawer for a stolen refrigerator, and if a refrigerator is the smallest thing listed on the warrant and you find a stolen pistol in a drawer, you shouldn't have been looking in that drawer, and the pistol stays right there and you can't make a case on it. Ever. Even if it's a murder weapon as well as a stolen pistol. But if you're looking for cocaine that's listed on your warrant and you find that stolen pistol, that's fine. Seize the pistol. The cocaine *could* have been in the drawer.

The smallest thing listed on our warrant was Helen French's door key. There's not much of a place a door key won't fit. This gave us a reasonably free hand on searching.

Root cellar. Mouldering baskets, heaven knows what could have been in them. A few very withered bulbs that could have been onions or tulips or just about anything else. Shelves of jars filled with blackened, withered green beans, peaches and apricots, tomatoes, corn relish, jellies and jams. Some of the jars had screw-on lids; others, once blue but changed now to a strange aqua-green shade, had glass lids held down by rusty clamps.

There was no evidence that anybody had been in there for just about as long a time as you wanted to name. There were no hidden cupboards, no doors blocked by shelves. Nothing. Nothing at all evidentiary. No little red rooms for Amityville horrors to hide in. Nothing except old used up domesticity.

If the kitchen hadn't still contained the stinking body fluids that had drained from two corpses, hadn't still been full of buzzing eager blue and copper flies, it would have seemed no more than an old-fashioned farmhouse kitchen with very few utensils remaining, and a sink full of half-empty cardboard coffee cups, many with cigarette butts in them. Climbing on chairs, we checked all the shelves. There were a few old dishes, all empty. There were a lot of cobwebs; there was a lot of dust. But there wasn't anything else.

The dining room was completely empty; the massive table and sideboard that should have filled it either had never existed or, more likely, had long since gone to one of the children's houses or to an antique shop. The semiconcealed floor-level door, about two feet square and covered with old wallpaper, that Aline spotted eagerly turned out to lead only to plumbing and wiring, and velvet-thick undisturbed dust made it obvious nothing had been hidden there.

The living room gave the impression that it had been carefully decorated during the later years of Queen Victoria and never touched since; nobody had been interested enough in the objects it contained to steal or even vandalize them, though teenagers had evidently hung out there some—there were interesting graffiti on the wall, a couple of roach clips on the mantel, and a small collection of used contraceptives in the fireplace. I suspected they'd been on the floor until Patrick Kelly came home and swept the small area he'd picked to occupy, because they lay in the midst of a heap of dirt, ashes, beetle carapaces, and other varied debris. The roach clips could have been Patrick's but I doubted it; he wasn't the marijuana generation.

But his partner—his killer—might be. On second thought I carefully collected the roach clips, lifting them with tweezers so as not to damage fingerprints and dropping them into a coin envelope. I wrote the date, the case number, the location found, the time, and added my initials, and then handed the envelope to Aline so she also could initial it.

Nothing else in that room. At least nothing that did us any good.

There was a camp bed in the parlor, with a sleeping bag on it. An open suitcase sat on the floor, with khaki work clothes and underwear and socks tossed into it unfolded. A plain white cotton laundry bag had a few dirty clothes stuffed into the bottom of it. On the floor between the suitcase and the laundry bag were a portable radio, a stack of newspapers, a couple of paperback Westerns, two *National Enquirer*s, and the October *Reader's Digest*. Which last was a little bit of a surprise.

We checked the suitcase. No laundry marks on any of the clothes; apparently he'd used a laundromat. Which was to be expected. A plastic package of disposable razors stuffed in the pocket of a flight bag otherwise filled with more dirty laundry. An old Bible. A dozen or so photographs. "Wonder who these are?" Aline asked, picking up one of them.

"I know who they are," I said. "This was Patrick's suitcase; I'm sure of that now." The photographs were of various members of the Kelly family. If I'd been asked yesterday I'd have said I probably couldn't recognize Sonny; I couldn't possibly recognize Susie. But I did recognize Sonny, standing with a happy grin on his face, his shirt open to expose a skinny hairless chest, and a softball in his hand; and I did recognize Susie, standing smiling beside Patrick in what was probably a wedding picture. I wondered why in the world a man would carry with him photographs of his brother whom he'd murdered, of the woman he'd murdered his brother over.

There were three color Polaroid snapshots of a child taken, apparently, in front of a school. A little girl, eight or nine years old, wearing the plaid uniform of a parochial school and carrying a red kangaroo bag. She was smiling shyly; apparently she didn't yet realize what was happening to her. "So that's what she looked like," I said, staring at the fourth photograph of the child—a different photograph. She was lying still, eyes open, staring sightlessly past the camera, wrapped in a pink blanket in the trunk of a car. Too much of a close-up to tell us anything about the car. But there it was, the blanket the lab had said we'd find.

The way the blanket was wrapped around her I couldn't see the ropes around her arms and legs. But I knew they were there.

Aline glanced at me. "You didn't know what she looked like? I thought you were the one who found her."

I reached for an envelope, carefully maneuvering the photographs by the edges so as not to damage fingerprints that might be on them. "I did find her."

After a minute Aline said, "Oh, shit. I didn't think of that. Yeah, I've been carrying pictures of her around for days. She was a cute kid. Wonder where the bastards stashed the camera?"

It wasn't in the parlor-cum-bedroom. The only other thing in it was an old-fashioned thundermug, sitting discreetly in one corner, quite clean. And some more graffiti, even more interesting and drawn in purple lipstick.

An attempt had been made to wash it off, but it had only smeared a little.

Upstairs, furniture had been removed from most of the bedrooms; apparently nothing had been left that anybody in the family had been able to use elsewhere. But it didn't appear that the mild vandalism had reached upstairs; there were no drawings on the walls. Pine shelves were slung together in a couple of rooms; there was an old badly rusted iron bedstead in one and a rotting cotton mattress rolled up on the floor in another. The small closets contained old shoes, old belts green with mold, an occasional out-of-style dress or shirt or pair of slacks hung carelessly on rusted wire hangers or slung on the floor. But nothing really. Nothing usable, nothing evidentiary.

The toilet had frozen in some forgotten winter; its empty porcelain bowl was cracked wide, and the top was gone from its rusty tank. A five-gallon jerrycan half full of water was sitting beside the sink; on top of it was a stiff dry washcloth, a can of shaving foam, a bottle of aftershave, a razor that seemed to have come from the pack downstairs. No toothbrush—he shaved but he didn't brush his teeth? No, a tooth bowl and a box of Polident sat on the window sill.

"How do you suppose the bathtub got that cruddy?" Aline asked, staring at the cobwebs over the rust.

"Lime," I said succinctly.

"But if you wash the tub the lime comes off."

"Not unless you wash it pretty often. These people

• 116 •

probably didn't have time to. You don't know much about dirt farming, do you?"

"Uh-uh," Aline said. "And that's only page one."

"I know. Page two is, you don't want to know."

"You got it."

And the radio came alive. Headquarters was calling me. It was fortunate I'd been carrying the radio from room to room with me.

"You put a lookout on a seventy-three Ford pickup registered to a Richard Mossberg?" the impersonal official voice asked.

"That's affirmative."

"Ten-four. Well, it's just been located."

"Yeah? Where?"

"Parked on the side of the road about two miles east of Shiloh Baptist Church. That's in the county. Nobody's in it, and the motor's cold. Truck's locked up and the gun rack is empty."

"Oh, shit," I said.

"*What* did you say on the air?"

"I said, oh, darn. Okay, get hold of somebody from the county and tell him I'll meet him there at—" I glanced at my watch—"three-thirty. That should give me time to finish up here."

"Ten-four. Clint Barrington will be working it for the county."

I know Clint Barrington, I've known him as long as I've been policing, and that's sixteen years and a little more. Clint was my first partner. That was before he went over to the sheriff's office. That might make it a little easier for me to keep track of—

"What's that all about?" Aline asked.

"I'll tell you later. Let's get on up to the attic; that's the last place we've got indoors, and I think we'll wait

· 117 ·

and hit the outbuildings tomorrow, and borrow some runarounds to help move things."

We were entering the attic when the dispatcher came back on the air to say, "Barrington'll be there at three-thirty. Layden from the county is standing by the car until one of you gets there."

"Ten-four." I set the radio down on a very dusty dressing table, its drawer front's ornately carved veneer now peeling away in huge splinters, its mirror broken in two with half of it gone and the corrugated cardboard backing crumbling away in dust. "It's nothing to do with this case," I said to Aline, "and I'm not really supposed to be on it anymore. But—"

"Then why are you going out there?"

"Because I feel guilty. The mother tried to report the kid missing Saturday and I wouldn't take the report."

"Why not?"

"Custody dispute. The father was legal. But he was supposed to have the kid back on Sunday night."

And then Aline said, "Gun rack was empty?"

"Yeah," I said. "The father's flat-ass broke and out of work and the mother's a complete dingbat. He could have decided he and the kid were best out of it. Stuff like that's happened before."

"Tell me about it," Aline said. "I had one a couple of weeks—what's that?"

"What's what?"

"That over there. Look. There's no dust on it, but what is it?" She pointed with her flashlight beam.

It was a red nylon windbreaker; on it was a logo—an outline map of the contiguous United States done in white, and printed across it also in white was one word: "SellAmerica."

"What in the heck is SellAmerica?" I wondered out loud.

"It's a boiler room," Aline said, also crouched over the jacket. "They sell magazines and stuff over the phone. I had to go talk to 'em once when a lot of boiler rooms were getting burglarized; that's how I know. They wanted us to warn all of 'em."

"What's to steal from a boiler room?"

"You'll never guess."

"So tell me."

"They stole the telephones. Forty-two of them from one place and seventy-three from another. And one place they stole all the city directories."

"Are you kidding me?"

"Uh-uh. I swear. They stole the telephones."

"Aline, what'd anybody do with forty-two stolen telephones? Or seventy-three?"

"Set up their own boiler room maybe? Or maybe sell them at a flea market. But the city directories too—"

"Set up their own boiler room," I agreed. "Are you going to pick that jacket up, or am I?"

"We better photograph it first."

"I guess so. I'll get our crime scene people out here—"

"Why bother? I've got a camera in my briefcase. I stuck it in your car."

And with the jacket photographed, with its location carefully noted and triangulated from a fixed object, we could move it and see that under it was a Tony Lama boot box, and some torn brown wrapping paper addressed in black marker, and no money at all.

The cross forest, which starts on the east coast in Virginia and the Carolinas, tapers out after going through East Texas. When you're heading west, it's so startling it grabs at the pit of your stomach like the feeling when you're trying to walk down one more stair in the dark but you're at the bottom and don't know it.

You're driving through the pine forest and then you crest a hill just outside of a little town called Commerce and all of a sudden the pines are gone and you're looking out at what looks like an endless expanse of rolling prairie. The blackland prairie, it's called, because the underlying rock is limestone from ancient seas, and limestone decomposes into a rich, black, horribly sticky earth. It looked so unlike what the settlers were used to seeing that they thought it was going to be useless land, until they planted in it and everything grew.

But it grows its own kind of barriers. There aren' any pines here, or at least not many, but a field of mesquite is an impenetrable barrier. Mesquites have beautiful, lacy leaves, and roots that go three-quarters of the way to China—they need them, because there's a lot less rain here than there is a couple of hundred miles to the east—and long, sharp thorns that can impale you in no time at all.

Technically there's not, so far as I know, any unsettled land around here. Technically it's all owned, technically it's all mapped—unlike the thousands of acres of swamp called the Big Thicket that aren't very far from here.

But that's only technical.

Hunters get lost here every year; even hunters who think they know the area and can't possibly get lost do it. Or maybe I should say especially hunters who know the area, because they're the ones who get superconfident and don't watch for landmarks.

Richard Mossberg was twenty-six years old and he'd lived—and hunted—in this part of Texas all his life, except when he was in the army. He shouldn't be that unwary; he should be able to find his way out.

That didn't mean he wasn't lost.

His blue Ford pickup truck sat completely off the tarred roadbed, on a gravel and clay shoulder. It was actually nearer two and a half miles from Shiloh Baptist Church, and the church of course was completely out of sight from where we were standing. The gun rack, as the dispatchers had said, was empty, but that didn't necessarily mean anything.

Because the report that the truck was locked was wrong. The truck wasn't locked. Both doors were unlocked.

So the guns might have been stolen.

For that matter he might not have had guns on the rack anyway; some people don't carry them all the time.

Or he might have decided to take the gun and go rabbit or squirrel shooting, although not many men would want to take a child with an upset stomach on a hunting expedition.

She might have gotten over the upset stomach fast, though. These things don't last long.

Clint Barrington wasn't there yet. He was supposed to be bringing a search warrant. With all the confusion of court decisions, we didn't want to take a chance on getting into the truck without one.

Aline looked at the trees and undergrowth, looked at the truck, looked at the roadside where the marked sheriff's car was just pulling out. "I don't see how you ever find anything out around here," she said. "I mean, what do you do when there's nobody to talk to?"

"He parked here Saturday," I said. "That's a starting point."

"How in the world can you tell—"

"I know how tar roads behave," I interrupted. "He left tire tracks. I know they're his because look, the tracks run right to his tires. He's—the truck is sitting in the tracks."

"Okay, but—"

"It was cool Friday. You don't leave tracks in cool tar, so it wasn't Friday he came here. It was cool Sunday and it's cool today. But there was a change in the weather Saturday. Saturday afternoon it got up to eighty-seven."

"More like a hundred and seven downtown," Aline agreed. "I mean, you just don't expect that in November."

"Here you do. At least every now and then. Anyway, tar heats up fast because it's black and it grabs every bit of heat and holds it. And hot tar softens. It holds tire tracks. If it's hot enough—like sometimes in the middle of the summer—it'll even hold shoe tracks temporarily, until it cools and then heats and softens again. So—he parked the truck on the last warm day, because we know the truck was seen in town since the last hot day before that one. He parked the truck in hot tar and the tar cooled and held the tracks. It hasn't been hot enough since then to soften them again. He parked here Saturday afternoon, probably around two o'clock in the afternoon because that's when it was the hottest, but certainly before four because that's when the cool front blew in. Well, I better not say that for sure, because tar will hold heat a while; maybe he could have parked here as late as four-thirty or five, but that's pushing it. I don't think it was much after three-thirty."

If it was before noon we should have been able to see the truck from the air. I didn't say that. It didn't matter, because I didn't see it from the air, or if I did I didn't notice.

"Three-thirty," Aline said. "Three-thirty Saturday.

Over two days ago." She looked around. "What's that way? Or that?" She gestured to both sides of the road.

"That way's a thin stretch of woods and then you get into a good-sized cow pasture, a dairy herd. Up on the other side of the pasture, on the side of the hill where you can't see it from here, is the farmer's house and his manager's house and several workmen's houses and the milking barn. He didn't go up there. Mangen doesn't allow hunting or fishing and he's got posted signs all over the place. The other way—" I wheeled slowly. "Woods. Just woods. Let me think, there's at least one big creek between here and the next highway—it's swampy that way; there's a lot of little branches all over the place. I used to play here when I was a kid. One of my cousins lived between here and the church. The house is gone now; somebody bought the land to put a factory on it and then didn't put in the factory."

"You serious? You used to play here? You don't mean by your cousin's house?"

"We used to play here. There's a—oh, when we were kids we thought it was the biggest swamp in the world. It wasn't, of course, but it is a real swamp and it's maybe seven, ten, acres around—the creek splits up into nine zillion little rivulets and you go back and forth between marsh and dry land in a step, and all summer long there's millions of wildflowers there, some of them so rare I never have been able to identify them in guidebooks. There's one place right at the edge of the swamp where the stream is running along on one level—regular ground level, I mean—and then all of a sudden you've got about an eight-foot drop into a little pool and the stream stays in this gullylike for quite a ways. The stream there is just a little too wide and deep to wade through, and when we were kids a tree had fallen across the pool below the waterfall and we crossed that way, scooting over the tree trunk, and one time my sister fell in. I was twelve and she was five. I could swim, but if I got into the pool I couldn't get out because the walls were so steep and all. I was trying to reach her with my hands, lying across the tree trunk, and I remember I was crying and I was scareder than she was."

"How'd she get out?"

"My uncle was with us that day. He pulled her out. He was a lot older than me. Fifteen, I think, or something like that. We were lucky there weren't any gar."

"Gar?"

"Alligator gar. Carnivorous fish. Where are you from?"

"Maine," Aline said, "and we don't keep carnivorous fish there. At least not except in the ocean. You think they're lost in that swamp, the man and the little girl?"

I shook my head. "I told you, it's just six or seven acres. I don't see how they could be."

"It seems to me anybody could get lost in a seven-acre swamp."

"Then you don't know how big an acre is. Or how little. Oh, *you* probably could get lost there, sure, being from the city, but he's an experienced hunter. There's no reason—"

"But—"

"He knows the area, Aline. Look, do you ever get lost in Dallas?"

"Well, yeah, kind of, sometimes. Dallas is a big place. But when I do I just drive around until I find a big cross street. I know all of them. And there's sure no big cross streets here."

"Actually there are, but you have to know how to find them. Look, first you find a stream, okay? There are a jillion streams and all you have to find is one. And then you follow it until you get to a bigger one. And if you follow it long enough, sooner or later it's got to cross a road, that's all."

"But what if it doesn't?"

"It's got to, if you keep following the stream long enough. All the streams around here are headed, eventually, for the Trinity River, and to get to the Trinity River they've got to cross roads."

"Oh. But how do you know which way to follow it?"

"Obviously, you follow the way it's going. I mean, you can tell which way the water's running. A blind man could tell which way the water was running."

Aline shook her head. "I wouldn't want to try."

"Aline, I got lost in that swamp, with some of my friends, when I was just ten years old. The oldest of the group was eleven. And we got back out. It was a long hot trip and we got out three miles up the road from where we wanted to be and had to walk back, but we got out with no trouble and we were every one home by supper. Seven acres isn't that big a space. He's not lost. There are a lot of things that might have happened, but he's not lost." I turned. "Here comes Clint."

Clint Barrington was pulling his car in behind mine. He looked at me with some displeasure. "Just exactly whose case is this?" he demanded.

"Oh, I know," I said guiltily, "but I'm just so darn worried about the kid."

"Worry about your own kid. You're too damn tired to stand up. Have you been puking again?"

"Who told you I'd been—"

"Just about everybody that knows I know you, that's all. Have you been puking again?"

"Morning sickness usually stops," I said with as much dignity as I could muster, "at about three months."

"So how far along are you?"

I had to stop and count. "Six months. About."

"So you're the exception. You're too damn tired to stand up. You don't have any sense anyway. You never did. When was your last day off?"

"Quit telling me I'm too tired to stand up! I am standing up!"

"Message from your captain. You are allowed to help me search this truck. Then you are to get your ass back home where it belongs and let me work my case. I was a cop before you were. I made detective before you did. I *trained* you, dammit! I know just as well how to work a missing person case as you do."

"Uh-huh," I said. "Did you get the search warrant? Or did you take off and forget it again?"

"Did I get the search warrant! Did I get the search warrant! One time in my life I forget a search warrant and you act like—" he was feeling in his coat pockets. "Yeah, I got the search warrant. See? Here's the search warrant. It says right here on the top, search warrant."

"Okay, Clint," I said, "you got the search warrant. So let's use it already." About that time I noticed Aline staring at us both.

Clint must have noticed too, because he said, "Ignore it. Ignore it all. We love each other, don't we, Deb?"

"Madly," I agreed. "Surely Aline can tell. Now let's get this truck searched. I want to go home."

There wasn't anything in the truck that didn't belong there. No suicide notes. No forgotten lunches. Nothing at all except a couple of hamburger wrappers and Coke cups and a box of Kleenex and a little girl's pink jacket.

Clint pushed his hat to the back of his head and looked out at the expanse of trees and underbrush and vines. "So I guess now I call out the posse," he said wearily.

"Posse?" Aline asked me in the car. "Come on! That sounds like something out of a John Wayne movie!"

"It's just a loosely organized group of volunteers who exist mainly to ride in parades," I said. "But they do come out when we need extra help for search parties and that sort of thing."

"So what happens if they get lost?"

"They won't. They know this area."

"You said Rick Mossberg knows this area."

"Rick Mossberg isn't lost. I told you that already. Whatever has or hasn't happened, that's not what happened. He didn't get lost."

Aline shrugged. "I need to phone my office about that CallAmerica jacket. You want to wait around while I do it, or just dump me at my car?"

"I've got to go into the office anyway and dictate a report onto the tape recorder. It won't get typed till tomorrow, but I hate to leave them overnight. So you might as well call from my office."

"She what? Okay, how? But—" Aline listened for a very long time, writing on a yellow legal pad as she listened. "Okay, you want me to head back in?"

"What's going on?" I asked.

Aline gestured at me for silence and went on listening. "But that doesn't make sense—okay, okay."

And after a while she hung up and turned to me. "Mrs. French shot herself this afternoon."

"She did what?"

"It would have made more sense if she'd OD'd or something; the doctor had prescribed her sleeping pills and stuff, but she shot herself. Deb, there weren't even any guns in the house. She went out and bought a pistol and went home and shot herself. Left some kind of crazy note saying it was all her fault and it takes blood to wipe out blood."

"Seven children," I heard myself saying.

"Yeah," Aline said, "seven children at home. Seven motherless children, now. Nobody seems to know any reason that makes sense. Oh, damn!" She sat down again, head in her arms hidden on Dutch's desk. "I've been on this since it started," she said, her voice half-muffled. "Since it was reported, anyway. Mrs. French seemed—upset, of course, from the very beginning, but she was holding herself together pretty well except—" She looked up again. "French belongs to some kind of off-the-wall church, they don't have a preacher or anything, but some guys from the church kept coming around with little nametags that said they were elders, and Mrs. French kept telling them she wasn't a member, she wasn't good enough to be a member, and that didn't make sense to me and I don't think it did to them either. And there were some ladies that kept coming over bringing her meals and looking after the children, and they kept telling her she shouldn't talk like that and none of it could possibly be her fault."

"It doesn't make sense to me either. My son belongs to that church now, and I go sometimes, and—"

"Oh, gosh, me and my big mouth—"

"No offense," I said hastily. "I know the church kind of looks off the wall, as you put it, but she—"

"I didn't understand it," Aline interrupted. "But anyway she stayed fairly calm until they found the body where they did—where you did. Then—French was all torn up, of course, but her—I never saw anybody fall apart the way she did, and that was when she started saying it was all her fault, all her fault, all because of her, it happened because of her, and he kept telling her that couldn't be true, there wasn't any way it could be, and she kept saying it was and he didn't understand and if he knew the truth he'd hate her—" Aline opened her purse and grabbed out a white envelope. "Look at this—no, wait."

She thrust the legal pad over to me, and that was when I realized she'd written down the text of the suicide note, in case it made some sort of sense at this end.

It was my fault Helen died. It was because of Sonny. I didn't mean Sonny to die but that was my fault too. And Helen died and Patrick died and I don't know who else but maybe this way it'll stop with me just like it started with me. It was my guilt that kept killing people over and over and over. It takes blood to wipe out blood. Jared, I'm sorry, I'm so sorry. I should have known I couldn't be free of what I did, of that kind of guilt. Take care of the children, find them a new mother, one that's clean.

Susanna

Aline took the note out of my hand and dumped photographs out onto the desk. A lot of pictures of the dead child, visibly a pretty little girl in snapshots, posed studio photographs. One group picture, Jared French, his wife, eight children—four boys, four girls—at least I assumed from the blue blanket that the baby was a boy. Aline gestured at the picture violently. "Even with Helen dead, look at what she had to live for! It doesn't make any sense at all!"

I picked up the group picture and studied it. "Susanna," I said. "Her name was Susanna?"

"Yes, why?"

I opened one of the grocery-sized evidence sacks we had used to collect evidence from the farm, and fished out one of the small evidence envelopes. Opening it, I nudged out the photograph in it, the old photograph of the man and woman from Patrick Kelly's suitcase. Putting the picture down beside the studio print Aline had dumped on the desk, I said, "Look."

Aline studied the two pictures; her eyes widened. "But you said—"

"Yeah. I said that was Susie Kelly. That was Patrick Kelly's wife, that was the woman Patrick Kelly killed his brother over. Susie Kelly is Susanna French. I know now why she shot herself—oh, that's horrible!" And I felt my stomach churning; I ran out of my office and toward the women's room as fast as I could run, and by the time Aline caught up with me I was crouched over a toilet, retching and sobbing with pity for—for everybody, everybody involved in this horrible nightmare, every one of them, even Patrick Kelly.

"Deb, let me take you home," Aline said. "This day's been too long—"

"I'll be okay." But I started retching again.

"Deb, either I'm taking you home or I'm calling your husband to come get you. Friends don't let friends drive—incapacitated."

Even I managed to laugh at that.

· 7 ·

When I woke up, somebody was banging around in the kitchen—Hal, I supposed, to judge by the raucous attempts at quiet. The refrigerator door slammed and Hal said, "Ooops!" Something—probably a bowl—clattered down rather loudly onto the table.

The patio door slid open, and Harry came in. "Get me the barbecue sauce," he whispered loudly.

The refrigerator door opened and then banged again. The patio door slid shut, riding rather loudly and squeakily in its aluminum tracks. A smell of chicken and charcoal came in.

Harry evidently was barbecuing chicken, while Hal made the salad. It was quite evident that Hal was making salad. He is the only person I have ever met who could make a lot of noise cutting iceberg lettuce with a paring knife.

Even Hal can't be too loud cutting tomatoes, though,

and I dozed back off again, waking with a start when I felt somebody licking my fingers.

It was, of course, Pat, half pit bull and half—at least so the vet thinks—Doberman. He is not what you would call a lap dog, though he tries awfully hard to plop down in the lap of anybody unwary enough to sit down in the yard, and when he is removed by the indignant (and squashed) victim he wags from the waist back to make up for his nearly total lack of tail. The fact that he is not allowed in the house comes to him as a constant indignity as well as a constant surprise, but every time the patio door is left open when nobody is looking he whooshes in and rushes, with great displays of joy, to whoever happens to be available.

That was why my hands were now being licked, very sloppily.

"Go away, Pat," I said sleepily.

Pat whined and, of course, did not go away.

I sat up and ran my fingers through my hair, stood up, and grabbed Pat by the collar to escort him to the patio door. "*Out,* mutt," I told him, and he whined heartbrokenly.

Although we acquired Pat only last spring, when he turned up wet and shivering on our doorstep, I can only assume that he must have become used—very early in puppydom—to people grabbing him by the collar or the chain to march him places he did not want to go. He is not a very smart dog in view of the fact that the average pit bull can pull a pickup truck—it has not yet occurred to him that he no longer has to go anywhere he does not want to go. Therefore when he is grabbed by the collar or leash, he meekly goes where he is told.

Harry, at the grill, turned around looking disappointed. "We were trying to surprise you," he said.

"Pat beat you to it," I said, turning the not very chastened dog loose in the yard.

"I thought Hal closed the door."

"He didn't."

Neither had I. I removed Pat from the house again, closed the patio door more carefully, and sat down on a lawn chair to watch Harry turning the chicken over about forty-nine times. One thing, it ought to be good. I had bought skinless boneless chicken breasts for a fancy dish I was going to make—never mind what it was; obviously I didn't do it—and Harry appropriated them for barbecue. Forget that they cost about three times as much as steak.

Obviously we did not eat outside. The picnic table is now used only for drinks, preferably drinks that Pat does not like.

Pat *loves* chicken.

At the moment I didn't, not much, but then I doubt I would have wanted to eat much of anything else I could think of. I needed to talk to somebody, and I thought back, wistfully, to the days when I was a good little girl and went to church every Sunday and had a pastor I could discuss things with.

But that gave me an idea. "Hal," I asked at supper, "if you needed to talk to somebody at church about a problem, who would you go to? I mean if it was a real problem?"

"Scoutmaster," he answered laconically. "Can I have some more milk? There'll still be enough left for breakfast."

"There better be. And it's *may* I, not *can* I. Hal, I mean if *I* wanted to talk to somebody. I don't have a scoutmaster."

He already had the refrigerator door open. He moves

about as fast as Pat, when food is in question. "I don't know," he said, head in the refrigerator. "Maybe the bishop."

"Hal, how long does it take you to get a carton of milk out?"

"Oh. Not long. There's a can of pears in here."

"I know. I put them there."

"Can we have them after supper?"

"I guess. Who's the bishop?"

"We got a new one."

"I know you got a new one. That's why I asked you who he is."

The Mormons, I should explain, have the most unusual church organization I have ever run across. On one level, it's arranged sort of like the Catholics, only instead of parishes they have wards and instead of dioceses they have stakes. The ward boundaries are very rigidly laid out and if you live in a ward you go to that ward's services, with no ifs, ands, or buts about it. Unlike the Catholics, they often have three or four wards meeting in one building on a staggered schedule, which means in effect that since this year Hal is going to church from nine in the morning to noon, next year he will go to church from eleven to two in the afternoon. But their most unusual feature is that they don't have any paid clergy. Instead they have a bishop—who is appointed, not elected—who sort of acts as pastor, along with two counselors who work with him.

Well, there's a lot more to it than that. For one thing the bishop doesn't give a sermon; several different people talk each Sunday, but that's about as much as I have figured out. The last bishop—he'd served five years, which I gather is the normal term—was the other six days of the week a delivery man for the Frito-

Lay company. I often wondered what the Frito-Lay people thought when Hal occasionally called their office wanting the bishop to call when he got in off his route, but I guess they must have gotten used to it.

I didn't know what the present bishop did because I didn't know who the present bishop was. Hal couldn't remember his name. I finally called the old bishop, who wasn't in, but his wife was able to refer me to the new bishop, who to my considerable surprise turned out to be a police sergeant I knew fairly well, a fellow by the name of Will Linden.

That helped; it meant I could talk to him without breaking security.

Will said he would come over and talk to me.

Harry said, "If he's going to ask me why I don't go to church, I'm leaving."

Hal looked reproachfully at Harry, and I said, "I don't think he will."

He didn't. He just listened to my explanation, which I hope was at least a little more coherent than my explanations tend to be, and then he said, "Deb, it doesn't sound to me like she was guilty of anything. At the most, maybe adultery, but that's certainly forgivable. And I'm not even sure about that. From what you tell me, I suspect all that really happened was mild flirtation, and even that she'd clearly repented of. She certainly had no reason to refuse to join the church, and no reason whatever to commit suicide. It's a shame she didn't just go talk to her bishop. See, the thing is, she was responsible for what she did—whatever that was— but not for anything anybody else did. I mean, I can certainly see how she'd feel bad, but there was just no reason—" He shook his head. "There was no reason, that's all."

"So now what happens?" I demanded resentfully. "I mean, her husband is this real religious guy. So is he going to go around thinking Susanna's going to hell or something? Is that church policy?"

Will shook his head again. "Church policy—in just about every church I ever heard of—says people shouldn't kill themselves. Or anybody else, for that matter. But we figure ultimately the whole thing's left up to the Lord to decide. And my guess is the Lord's going to decide Susanna French has already suffered quite enough and then some."

"And that's what French's bishop is going to tell him?"

"Quit being so suspicious, Deb," Will said. "That's what French's bishop is going to tell him. And would have told her, if she'd given him a chance."

"Okay," I said, not feeling very satisfied. Obviously he knew what he was talking about. But that didn't make me any happier. My old pastor would undoubtedly have said Susanna French was going to hell. That was why I quit going to church. His God sounded mean and vicious to me, and I don't believe God is mean and vicious.

I certainly hoped Will was right, that his God would see it my way. Because I didn't like this at all. A child dead apparently for no reason at all, and now the mother of that child—and seven other children—also dead for what seemed no reason. None of it made sense to me. And I'm to the age that I like things to make sense, although in honesty I should be able to admit I'm to the age where I know things usually don't make sense.

Will got up to leave. Of course he politely invited me to church before going. Of course he invited Harry too, but he did it so politely that even Harry didn't manage to find a way to take offense. Then he left, after reminding Hal he'd pick him up in the morning for seminary.

Rats, I thought. Rats, rats, rats, rats, rats.

Cravenly leaving my husband and son with the dishes after they'd already cooked the supper, which was supposed to be my job, I called Pat and took off on a long walk.

We gathered in the muster room the next morning, after the uniform division had finished holding muster, because there were too many of us to fit easily into any conference room in the detective division. Captain Millner announced himself moderator of the meeting, and nobody seemed inclined to argue with him, so apparently Captain Millner was moderator of the meeting. He looked first at Otto Castillo. "What've you got so far, Castillo?" he asked.

Castillo, sitting with about six other postal inspectors, stood up. Glancing occasionally at them, occasionally at me, and occasionally at his clipboard, he said, "Patrick Kelly was a Fort Worth city policeman until he shot and killed his brother Harrison Kelly approximately twenty-six years ago. He did ten years for manslaughter and was released from prison, on parole, sixteen years ago. He found a job working in Dallas as a makeready man for an automobile agency; he stayed with that one for fourteen years and then it bankrupted. He was out of work approximately two months. He went to work, again as a makeready man, for French's Chevrolets and he worked there until about five months ago."

I sat up straight, as Castillo glanced meaningfully at me. Jared French had told both Castillo and me that he had never heard of a Patrick Kelly. Admittedly it was a large agency, but if Kelly had worked for him two years French ought to know him. So why didn't he—or why did he say he didn't?

Castillo went on talking. "At that time he turned sixty-two and took early retirement and returned to the family farm to live on Social Security. He's been living there five months. He had a fifty-seven Chevrolet he'd left at the farm while he was in prison. He was reconditioning it the last two years he was in Dallas and he's been working on it some more since he got here; that apparently was the car that was burned. We've been checking all his known associates. So far as we've been able to determine he never remarried—Susie, the woman over whom he shot his brother, divorced him during the trial. We can't find anybody who admits to seeing or hearing much of him since he retired; apparently he's been keeping to himself, somewhat of a loner. Everybody we've talked to says he seemed to be sorry about the fight with his brother, did not seem resentful about the prison sentence, and refused to talk about the whole situation. We haven't followed up on the relationship with French; that's a Dallas PD matter. That's as far as we've gotten so far and we plan to go on following that line right now, under the assumption that somebody he knew shot both him and our mail carrier."

"Okay. Ms. Brinkley?"

Aline stood up and introduced herself, somewhat more politely than yesterday. "We'd already gotten the automobile agency relationship, before I headed over here yesterday; as soon as Kelly was identified we went and checked employment records there. Everybody we talked to that knew him in Dallas said he got along with people. Obviously as a makeready man he wouldn't

· 138 ·

have had any contact with French personally—that's really a large agency—except maybe at the company Christmas party or something like that, and we didn't find any evidence that would tend to contradict that. But yesterday Deb and I found something that we'll need to get officially verified, but it looks like it's going to be the real link and probably at least part of the motive. Deb, would you—"

Feeling ridiculously self-conscious—although I was probably wrong, I at least felt that every eye in the room was on my maternity slacks and smock top instead of my face, and everybody was wondering what I thought I was doing instead of listening to my report—I stood up. "We found some pictures in Patrick Kelly's suitcase that I recognized. One of them was of his former wife, the one he shot Sonny—his brother—over. I ought to mention I knew the family fairly well when I was a kid. His wife's name, as you've heard, was Susie. Then a while later Aline—Detective Brinkley—showed me a picture of French's wife Susanna. It's the same woman."

"You sure of that, Deb?" Millner asked quickly. "It's been a long time."

"It's been a long time but I'm sure. Of course we need to get documentary evidence."

"Get it. Today."

"Can I put somebody else on it?" I asked hopefully. "Aline and I searched the house yesterday but today we wanted to get some runarounds and go back out and search the outbuildings and barns and so forth."

"We'll put Dutch on it then."

I forebore to point out that Dutch was supposed to be looking for Candy Mossberg, who had or had not been kidnapped by her father. It didn't much matter anyway;

after the truck turned up, the county had pretty well taken over the case, and at my request, Harry was taking to the air today in a company helicopter—he's a test pilot for Bell Helicopter—to see if he could spot them from the air. So Dutch might as well go try to find out where and when Susie Kelly had become Susanna French.

Millner called on another postal inspector, a man I slightly knew named David Lee. "I've been tracing the ransom money," Lee said. "It was mailed from the post office substation off Alpha Road, behind Valley View Mall in Dallas, and it was delivered here by a mail carrier named Cooper to Box Two-twenty-J, which doesn't exist—it was put up temporarily for that one day. We do still show a Two-twenty-J on the post office files, and it's still listed as belonging to Joe Kelly, but Joe Kelly's been dead a good twenty-five years and it should have been changed to Patrick Kelly when he inherited the farm. But he never bothered to change it, and best as I can tell from our files nobody was getting mail there from the time Joe was buried until the time Patrick moved out there five months ago, unless maybe Patrick lived there a little while before killing his brother."

"He did," I interposed. "He was living there while he was married to Susie."

"Thanks. Anyhow, if he did—and I guess from that he did—then the box stayed in his father's name. Patrick Kelly, since he got here, has been getting his mail at a post office box. We've got a mail cover on it and so far—of course this covers only the few days since his body was found—all he's gotten has been the gas bill and the electric bill. No letters, no magazines, no nothing. Social Security says his check is being direct-deposited into his bank—that's First Security—and I got a court order to have a look at his checking account. He's getting—been getting, that is—a Social Security check and he's been writing checks to the electric company and the gas company and the filling station and the grocery store. A few checks to an auto parts firm and a few to a farm supply store and one big one to a water-well firm. I checked with them, and they said they'd cleaned out the well and installed a new pump. So that's it, so far as we've got. Nothing unexpected or unusual."

"Anything else?" Millner asked. "You do all know Deb and Aline found the box and wrapping paper French used to mail the ransom, don't you?"

They all knew that. They all knew we didn't find any money.

Millner asked the one Ranger in the room if he had anything to add, and he shook his head. "I've been working with the postal inspectors so far."

Millner took his glasses off and meditatively scratched the bridge of his nose. "So we've got a motive for—everybody does know that French's wife shot herself yesterday?"

Apparently everybody knew.

"We've got a motive, of sorts, for Kelly to kidnap the French child—he might have blamed Susanna for Sonny's death and his own term in prison, although we don't have anybody that actually says he did. Apparently Susanna shot herself because she believed that was the motive for the kidnapping and couldn't live with the resultant feelings of guilt. All that would be just fine if Kelly was alive for us to arrest and question him. But Kelly's dead, and most likely whoever killed him also killed Bassinger, and that's who we need to find. Now what I want to know is, are we any forwarder on that?"

Nobody said anything. Apparently nobody was any forwarder on that.

"Deb, you said Sunday you were going to talk to Kelly's brothers and sisters. How far did you get?"

"Lantana and Billy Jack. That's all. Oliver's dead—"

"When did Oliver die?"

"Oliver's been dead five years, don't you remember?"

"Frankly, no. And since not all these people know the whole family—" (that was an understatement, I thought—) "why don't you explain?"

I did not appreciate being singled out to stand up again. "Well, Patrick had three sisters," I said. "Audrey and Roma and Lantana. Audrey and Roma both got married and moved away and Lantana married Billy Jack Turner and they live in the Birdville area." I was talking about old times; I automatically used the old term and then had to correct myself. "I mean the Haltom City area. And he had three brothers, Richard and Oliver and Harrison. Oliver's dead—Captain Millner, you ought to remember that, he ran into a bridge abutment DUI on Christmas Eve five years ago."

"Oh yeah," Millner said. "Totaled out a fifty-seven Chevy. I ought to remember the car, even if I didn't remember him."

Apparently I was the only person in the room who remained unaware of the importance of '57 Chevrolets. I needed to make the time to learn a little more about them. But right now I had to talk about the Kelly brothers.

"Okay, so Oliver's dead and Harrison of course is dead, because he's the one Patrick shot. And Richard was career army and last I heard he was a sergeant stationed in Germany and due to retire and so I suppose he's retired by now, because that was a while back, but he didn't move back into this area so far as I know."

"Okay," Millner said, "so you've talked to Lantana; and Oliver and Sonny and of course Patrick are dead; and that leaves Audrey and Roma and Richard to locate. Locate them."

"But—"

"The post office is following up Patrick's known associates. Dallas is working the Dallas end of it. You and Aline are going to search the rest of the farm this morning, and after you do that, Aline can go do whatever Dallas wants her to do and you can go find Audrey and Roma and Richard. And Audrey and Roma's husbands and Richard's wife, for that matter. Whatever it takes to find them."

"But the FBI can find Richard a lot faster than I can."

"That's true," FBI agent Dub Arnold agreed. "I'll get on that. Sergeant Richard Kelly, last known duty station in Germany, you don't know how long ago, and I don't suppose you know his service number?"

"Surely you jest."

"That's what I figured. We'll find him."

"Anything else before we head in our own directions?" Millner asked.

"Yeah," Aline said, "the jacket."

"What jacket?"

"The box and stuff the ransom was mailed in. When we found the box and all, they were wrapped in a Sell-America jacket. Last night I put my office onto finding out who that jacket belonged to."

"How do you figure to find that out?"

"The jacket probably belonged to Patrick anyway," Castillo said.

"You just got through listing the places he worked," Aline pointed out, "and they didn't include Sell-America."

"What is SellAmerica anyway?" Millner asked.

Aline explained, and Castillo said, "Well, if he was out of work he might have worked there for a while, to fill in."

"He might have. But then he might not. Anyway my office is trying to find out. I'll call before we break up and see if they've got anything, in case somebody else needs to know."

There is a telephone on the wall of the muster room. Aline spent most of the next five minutes listening; then she returned and said, "Patrick Kelly never worked for SellAmerica, at least not in Dallas, and trying to find out who the jacket belonged to is going to be the pits. First, they were given out only once, and that was in April and May three years ago. According to the manager—one of our detectives spent several hours talking to her last night—something like that would come in a humongous box from New York, which is where their corporate headquarters is, and then the managers would use them as sales promotional aids to make people work harder. Supposedly, anyway. They'd give out one jacket a night to whoever sold the most magazine subscriptions that night—"

"That ought to be easy enough," Millner interrupted. "Surely they'd keep records of that."

"Yeah, except that's not all they do. They also have goofy contests like 'Guess the Name of the Movie,' which I gather they play sort of like hangman only different, and you get to guess a letter every time you sell a magazine, and whoever guesses the name of the movie will get a jacket. That kind of games. And nobody kept any kind of record about who got those jackets. And their employees tend to come and go with considerable frequency—there'll be a cadre of people who stay for a while, and then about two-thirds of the people will turn over constantly. Carl said the best the manager could figure out there'd been about a hundred and thirty people working there during some part of the period the jackets were given out. Carl asked for a list, but that was two managers ago and the current manager isn't sure she can find it. She says she might have to get it from corporate headquarters if it's in with the old payroll records, or she might have to see if the old secretary that quit about two months ago knows where it's going to be."

Into the ensuing silence, one postal inspector muttered, "Shit!"

"Shit is right," Millner replied. "Well, let's hit the road. Deb, you said you needed some runarounds?"

"Yeah, a couple."

"I'll call over to the jail."

"Just a minute," Aline said, as people began to stand and reach for their jackets, "there's one more thing."

"What's that?" Millner asked resignedly.

"There's another SellAmerica office in Arlington. Obviously anybody living in either Dallas or Fort Worth could work there easily enough. Jay called out there and they said they'd never employed a Patrick Kelly, but he didn't get out there to find out how many people they would have had during the period the jackets were being given out. He's going out there tonight. One more thing the Dallas manager said was, that besides the jackets they give out baseball caps and key rings and all kinds of junk, and for long-time employees they give out more expensive stuff. So—"

"So if you're questioning anybody and notice anything with a SellAmerica logo you want to talk real close to that person," Millner finished for her.

"Right," Aline said, looking slightly ruffled.

"Captain," I asked, "what about Candy Mossberg?"

"The county's on it now," he told me. And that, of course, was all he could tell me.

Aline and I headed for the jail.

The runarounds, dressed identically in dingy white shirts and dingy white trousers with a gray stripe down the outside of each leg, sat in the back seat of the car and looked pleased. One of them was a large black man in his late forties; named Leander, he had solemnly explained to us that he was just fine most of the time until that neighbor of his went to driving him nuts, and then he went out and got drunk and got arrested and got to spend a month in jail for public intox and then he didn't have to listen to that neighbor for a whole entire month, but he was due to get released tomorrow and then he'd have to go back to listening to that neighbor all over again. "Didn't you ever think of moving?" Aline asked.

"Oh, no'm, I never *would* find a better garden spot than I gots now."

The other, a lively blond nineteen-year-old named David, couldn't quite understand what he was doing in jail, he said; he'd been living with these people and they were real nice people and he'd promised he was going to pay them rent just as soon as he found a job, only for some reason they got tired of him living there after about six months and they told him to pick his clothes off the floor and move out and so he moved out and went to sleeping in the park and that wasn't nobody's business but his if he wanted to sleep in Trinity Park and mooch cigarette money from people only somebody complained and then he got arrested for vagrancy and sentenced to thirty days and that didn't make sense because he was looking for a job, honest he was, and he worked at Burger King for two whole days and it was dumb to fire him just for having a catsup fight.

He'd dropped out of high school and left home at sixteen, and the best I could figure out he'd been on the bum ever since. But he was big, husky, and cheerful, and delighted to have a day away from the jail.

Having two prisoners in the back seat tended to curb discussion between Aline and me, so it was a silent drive until we turned down the road leading directly to the farm. Then Leander, in the back seat, said, "Miss Deb, ain't this the Kellys' place?"

"Yes, it is. You know it, I gather?"

"Yas'm. Ol' Mistuh Joe, he used to make some mighty fine shine." He chuckled reminiscently. "Mighty fine shine."

"Well, if you find any, leave it alone."

"Yas'm," he said resignedly.

Interesting, I thought. I hadn't known that. I wondered if my parents had. Anyway, it had nothing to do with the present situation.

There was a barn, almost falling down, and a garage, not much better. There was an outhouse, long since abandoned and totally overgrown with honeysuckle vines. There was a long shed housing an old tractor, the tractor motor in pieces on a sheet of newspaper on the ground. I checked the date. Only eight days old. Interesting.

A hundred-gallon drum of gasoline—new—was sitting in one corner of the shed, with several gallon cans of motor oil beside it.

Apparently this was the tractor that had been used to mow the yard. But if it was, it hadn't stood up very well to the strain. Which, I suppose, explained why nobody had finished mowing the yard.

Searching the outbuildings was a long, hot, tiring waterhaul. With one exception, there was nothing that seemed to have anything to do with the case. The outhouse contained a nest of spiders and a small rattlesnake, which Leander offered to club to death but David wanted to let alone. I agreed the snake didn't seem to be bothering anyone and could be safely left to its self-appointed task of rat-catcher; furthermore, I added, if it did have to be destroyed Aline or I would take care of the matter.

"Speak for yourself," Aline said, with a slight shudder. It seems she regards snakes the same way I regard spiders.

The barn door was nailed shut with rusty old nails; so were all the windows, so we had to have David and Leander pry the door open. It contained nothing at all except some very far gone hay—it wouldn't even do now as mulch—some old feed drums, and several very fat rats. Apparently the rattlesnake hadn't extended its jurisdiction this far.

The garage contained fragments of twenty or thirty old bicycles. It also contained several fan blades, a number of broken chairs, portions of four motorcycles (the newest was a 1949 Harley; judging from its degree of decrepitude, it may not have been running since

1950), three gasoline cans with the bottoms rusted out, fourteen window screens (ripped) in wooden frames, a yellow Formica kitchen table with rusted legs, a lot of old soft drink bottles, an assortment of metal drums and copper tubing that could very easily be reassembled into a still, a lot of broken glass, and a lot of dead leaves and tree limbs which had presumably fallen in through the roof, which had also fallen in. Among the debris we found one large new rural mailbox labeled 220-J. The mailbox was hidden under three large fruit jars which, Leander informed us, Joe had used to hold shine. All three jars were sealed shut and contained a clear fluid. Leander looked at them wistfully, and I picked up a chair leg and broke all three bottles, after discovering it was impossible to open them any other way to pour the contents out.

Judging from the smell, two contained shine. The third contained turpentine.

In the long shed someone had been working on the tractor; there were tools, more or less neatly stashed in a metal tool chest, beside it. But there were other, smaller parts that indicated someone had also been working on a car. I reminded myself that on leaving here I wanted to have another look in the burned 1957 Chevrolet, to see whether there was any indication it could conceivably have been the kidnap vehicle.

Would anybody dare to use that conspicuous a car to commit a crime? Would anybody have noticed it if they had?

Of course the Dallas police hadn't asked the people in the vicinity of the school if they'd seen a 1957 Chevrolet; they'd just asked about unusual vehicles, and on a Dallas city street in the ritzy part of town not much of anything is very unusual, from a Model T Ford to a Rolls Royce Silver Cloud.

We took the runarounds back to jail, where David ardently assured us how wonderful it had been to help us and how glad he'd be to help again if they had any way, any way at all, to use him.

"We'll keep that in mind," I promised solemnly.

After the door shut behind him Aline burst out laughing. "He's got the makings of a fine con man."

"To the manner born," I agreed. "I'm going over to the pound to have a look at that car. Want to come with me?"

"Yeah, sure," Aline agreed, "but let me make a pit stop first."

As I had been making pit stops all day, I couldn't very well argue. Detouring by my desk, I found a message to call the FBI.

"You know that Sergeant Kelly you wanted us to locate?" Dub Arnold said. "Didn't take much locating. He's dead."

"Dead?"

"Yeah, he died at the army base in Frankfurt, Germany, three years ago. Heart attack, just about six weeks before he was due to retire."

"Thanks for checking, Dub," I said.

That left two Kellys still to locate, Audrey and Roma. That was going to be harder, because they were both— at least presumably—married and hence no longer named Kelly. I know Roma had married Carl Gilbert, but Audrey? I had no idea.

I'd get on that tomorrow. It had somehow gotten to be three-thirty. We just had time enough to look at the pound.

The pound is located in the far north part of town,

not far from the river, and the blackened wreckage of the 1957 Chevrolet had been towed there Saturday afternoon. There it still sat; the interior was gutted, but the engine and the trunk had hardly caught at all. Both had been popped open from the heat of the flame, or had been popped open by firemen wanting to be sure the fire was dead out; either way, both sat gaping open.

If they had moved the stuff from the trunk to the interior before starting the fire it might not all have burned. The pink blanket—if there was one—would be gone, of course, but there might be charred fragments of it. A door key, the metal pieces of the kangaroo purse, might show up even if the flammable parts of the purse had burned.

But there wasn't any metal key or any metal pieces of the kangaroo purse; from all Aline and I could find, getting ourselves thoroughly filthy in the process, the interior was preternaturally clean. There was only one thing in it that wasn't a part of the car itself.

One thing, in pieces. But that one thing was very, very interesting.

In the right front floorboard, the metal part of a .410-gauge shotgun shell.

In the back floorboard, very small shot, like BBs, that almost certainly had come from a .410-gauge shotgun shell.

The medical examiner's office and the lab had listed a .410-gauge shotgun as the most likely murder weapon for both Kelly and Bassinger.

With all that to go on, Aline and I were able to work out, despite the fire, the places the shot had hit the back seat. The shot pattern hadn't spread far, but it had spread far enough to make it virtually certain that the gun had discharged in the front seat, and the shot pattern outlined a man sitting in the back seat.

"It was an accident," Aline said. "He didn't mean to kill him. The gun was sitting in the front seat, or more likely they were passing it from one seat to the other, and it discharged. Shotguns'll do that sometimes. I had a case once—oh, never mind the war stories."

"We've all had them," I agreed, remembering the startled look on the dead face of a child whose brothers had been playing with their father's shotgun. The best we could work out, the gun had been being tossed from one to another, and it had actually discharged in the air.

"I was beginning to read it as accident anyway," I added. "But if it wasn't deliberate murder, the whole thing was incredibly stupid, because anybody would be able to find Patrick Kelly, and Patrick Kelly—if he were still alive—would have told the rest of it without much leaning."

"So we know now we're hunting a stupid person," Aline said. "Did you send for the lab?"

"Yeah, they're supposed to be on the way. We can look in the trunk again while we're waiting, anyway."

The trunk contained exactly what it had contained last time I looked in it, a spare tire and a jack. And it was totally unburned. There wasn't any place for a pink blanket and a red purse to hide.

"I don't think this is it," Aline said.

"I don't either," I agreed, and turned to look at the entrance to see if the lab truck was anywhere near.

Turned, and turned again to be sure the forest green 1957 Chevrolet was still behind me, still burned, because directly in front of me, in a line going toward the back of the pound lot, was a second forest green 1957 Chevrolet, completely intact. "What the hell?" I asked, and saw Aline's mouth as agape as mine was.

And I headed for the office.

"It was towed in here, I don't know, I'd have to look at the records, maybe Sunday night," the pound keeper said five minutes later. "Officer on it—let's see—is Shea. He said there wasn't any stolen and they couldn't contact the owner, so—"

"I should have known," I said. "I'm going to kill Danny Shea. I swear I'm going to kill Danny Shea."

"I've really got to meet this Danny Shea," murmured Aline demurely, deliberate malice in her voice.

"Shea got the VIN and had me run it for stolen," Vinson said, "and it came back no stolen."

"1957 automobiles didn't *have* VINs," Ben Isaacs told him.

"They didn't? But I ran—"

"What you ran was a motor number, not a VIN. Motors, Vinson, are interchangeable; that's why the VIN system was established. Did you think to run the motor number for registration? That is SOP, isn't it? Or doesn't anybody around here read the *Standard Operating Procedures* anymore?"

"Of course I ran it! It came back registration canceled."

"Do you still have the paperwork?"

"Of course. That's SOP, too," Greg Vinson added, slightly spitefully.

"Run the registration again."

But he didn't have to. When Vinson got out the blue vinyl notebook the paperwork was in, the first line said, "Registration canceled." The second line said, "Prior registration Patrick Kelly, Kelly Road, Fort Worth, Texas." It gave the number of the license plate that should have been on the car.

The registration had been canceled on Saturday,

when a 1957 Chevrolet bearing those license plates was found burned on a country road just inside Fort Worth, Texas.

"This is impossible," Vinson muttered, staring at the two messages.

"You're telling me," Isaacs muttered, taking them out of his hand.

"Look, this flippin' car can't be burned and not burned at the same time," Vinson said, snatching them back.

"It sure can't," I agreed, looking over his shoulder. "Which means somebody has worked a real sweet con on us."

"He might not have meant to kill him when he did," Aline asserted, "but he sure as hell meant to kill him. He had to."

"Just a minute, I'm thinking," I said. "To start with, they used *his* car—"

"Whose car?" Vinson yelled. "For what? What the hell are we talking about?"

"We don't know who," Aline yelled back. "We're talking about the kidnapping." I was glad nobody had ever told her not to be rude to somebody in a wheelchair. Sometimes Vinson needed somebody to get rude to him. Especially when he was rude first. But I wasn't the one to do it.

"He—whoever he is—used his car for the kidnapping, I'm trying to say," I went on, "and somehow the gun went off by accident and he knew he couldn't get rid of the bloodstains so he put his plates, I mean he put Patrick's plates, on his car so when we found the burned car, which was his, we'd think it was Patrick's. Then he abandoned Patrick's car downtown. So that means the burned car has to be his. Now when we run the VIN—"

"It hasn't got—"

"Okay, Ben, I mean its motor number."

"Yeah, but that's kind of funny, two identical cars, that old," Aline objected.

"You got any better ideas?" I challenged. "They're there, aren't they?"

"Yeah, that's true. But if he'd used his car for the kidnapping we'd have found Helen's purse and the pink blanket in it. And we didn't."

"That's not necessarily so," I argued. "The purse might have been left in the street in Dallas and just been stolen."

"But the pink blanket didn't. And we know the pink blanket was there. We saw pictures of it."

They could have thrown it away. But I didn't say that; anyway, even if they had, there should be at least a little pink fluff, maybe hairs of the child's head, in the trunk.

The crime scene people would take care of that. They were already out at the scene. And all we had to do was call them to get the motor number too.

But I wanted to go back out there and look inside. And for that I needed a search warrant.

I was going to be late getting off again.

The red kangaroo purse containing the inhaler was in the trunk of Patrick Kelly's car. So was one of Helen's black kiltie loafers, still wrapped in the pink blanket they could have used—but didn't—to cover her pathetic little corpse.

So Helen French's kidnapping and Patrick Kelly's death had not taken place in the same car.

But the registration on the motor in the burned 1957 Chevrolet came back canceled, and this one had been canceled in 1961, when the car was totaled in the wreck that had killed its owner. It had been towed to a wrecking yard in Tyler and there, presumably, it remained, being parted out.

The inspection sticker might have had the original motor number on it, but the inspection sticker had been neatly razored off before the car was set afire. Which said it probably *did* have the original motor number on it, and that was what we'd have been able to trace to the owner.

Without the original motor number, without the license plates, there wasn't going to be any documentary way to trace the ownership of this car. That meant we were going to have to go at it other ways. And I wasn't real sure, yet, what those other ways were going to be.

One thing I was certain of was that Aline had been wrong in what she'd said at the pound.

We weren't looking for somebody stupid. We were looking for somebody smart.

Somebody very damned smart indeed.

· 8 ·

"IT WOULD HAVE BEEN a real sweet con if it had worked," I told Harry. "I just keep thinking about how it would all fit together. I really think they might have gotten away with it, if they'd been careful enough."

"Oh?" Harry said. He was sitting at the kitchen table; supposedly, he was helping me with the dishes, but in fact he'd decided to get out of my way. I didn't blame him; I was scurrying around like a mad thing while thinking out loud. Besides that, the multicolored striped dish towel he had now for some reason hung around his neck was too wet to use, and I'd grabbed another one. "How do you read it, then?" he asked.

"First they kidnap Helen in Kelly's car, not in—whoever's. I mean whoever owned the other car. I guess I'll call him X for now because I've got to call him something to talk about him."

"Okay, they kidnap Helen in Kelly's car, not in X's,

then what?" At least I think that's what Harry said. When I start thinking out loud I expect encouraging noises, but I rarely notice what's actually being said.

"Well, at that point they'd be pretty sure French was intimidated enough that he woudn't call in the police at once. Look, Harry, if Kelly didn't really know French there had to be somebody in it that did, to be able to read his character that well, because most men would call the police as soon as the child went missing, no matter what the kidnapper said. But they seemed to be sure he wouldn't. I think they didn't mean Helen to die, but dead or alive there was always the chance she could leave something in the car—hair, fiber, that kind of thing—but they seemed to be able to assume the police wouldn't be called in at least until after the ransom was delivered. I don't know why they were able to assume that, but from the way this was set up it's pretty obvious they did assume it."

"Deb," Harry said, "I hate to tell you this, but I haven't the slightest idea what you're talking about. What does the police not being called in have to do with Helen leaving something in the car? I think you've left out a connecting loop or something."

"No I haven't." I pulled out a chair and sat down across from him. "There are all kinds of books available about kidnapping—I told you about that case in Australia they finally cleared because of the kind of leaves that were on the boy's body."

"Sure, the books are available, but what makes you think they read them?"

"If you were going to plan a kidnapping wouldn't you read books about it?"

"I wouldn't plan a kidnapping."

"But if you were going to—"

Harry shrugged. "Okay, I'll play your game. Yes, I suppose I'd read books about it. But you already told me Patrick used to be a police officer himself."

"Sure, he was a police officer when all you needed to be one was a thirty-eight and a billy club. I know him. Knew him. I knew his family. They're decent people in general but they're not *smart* people. And somebody involved in this case was smart. There was planning on it, good planning—planning so good that when we first saw it we couldn't see any evidence of the planning at all."

"What makes you think—"

I went right on talking, ignoring Harry's expression of frustration. "Look at it. Finally French would report the kidnapping—anybody would assume he finally would, although if they'd delivered Helen back alive and made sufficiently real-sounding threats they might have managed to get away clean without him ever reporting it. But if they had it figured the way it looks to me like they did, he wouldn't have reported it until after Helen was returned; as it was—"

"I'm trying to see it your way," Harry said. "Okay, so Helen is returned alive and French finally reports the kidnapping and of course he tells the address he mailed the ransom to, because there's no way in the world they could count on him forgetting it even if he didn't write it down. And as soon as the address was given somebody would just go trotting right out to Box Two-twenty-J and find out where it belonged, even if the box was gone by then, and—"

"And we would all go haring out to the farm and there wouldn't be anything there," I said.

"What?"

"There wouldn't be anything there. Sure, there'd be a

fifty-seven dark green Chevrolet there, and Kelly would say, 'Mister, I don't know what you're talking about, but you're sure welcome to look in my car,' and we'd look, and there'd be *nothing there at all*."

"What?"

"Because it wouldn't be his car. It'd be X's car with Kelly's license plates on it. And Kelly would say something like, 'Mister, I don't know what kind of game somebody's playing, but I get my mail at the post office, and there's not even a Box Two-twenty-J out there. There used to be when my daddy was alive, but there sure isn't now. Mister, somebody's framing me.' And we go and look and he's right, there's no Box Two-twenty-J."

"So Helen describes everything to you and you get a search warrant and go and search the place and find the mailbox in the garage and the wrapping paper and the boot box in the attic. Come on, Deb, you can do better than that."

"They wouldn't have put that stuff there if things hadn't gone wrong. They'd have disposed of all of it somewhere else. And I don't think they'd have taken Helen to the farm at all if she hadn't died; I think they'd have taken her somewhere else entirely."

"Whether she saw the farm or not, she saw them. That's for certain. You told me they took pictures of her in front of the school. And nobody's going to be sitting in front of an elementary school in downtown Dallas in the middle of the day taking pictures and wearing masks."

"True, but she was a young child and she'd have been scared out of her mind. All they'd have had to do is change their clothes and maybe get a different haircut or shave off a beard or mustache and she'd never make them. Harry, no lab in the world could have proved she was transported in that car because she wasn't. She was transported in the other car. We couldn't have proved the ransom went to the farm, because anybody could have put that box up for one day and then taken it back down. We never could have proved anything except by the word of one small, frightened child. They were using the real trail to lay a false trail, and it very probably could have worked, if Helen hadn't died. I even think they could have pulled it off even after Helen did die, if they hadn't been so careless with that shotgun that Kelly wound up dead too."

"Maybe so," Harry said. His voice sounded highly dubious.

"But I think they panicked completely when Helen died," I added. "I mean, really—Helen died two or three days before Patrick Kelly did, yet they just left her in the pantry. A corpse in the pantry, Harry, can you imagine how that place got to smelling?"

"I wish I couldn't," Harry said. "I smelled enough of that in Vietnam to last me a lifetime and then some."

"And it wouldn't have taken it long to get that way. If they'd had any kind of sense at all they'd have buried her in the woods somewhere, and most likely we never would have found her. That's why I'm reading it as panic."

"Well, that makes sense," Harry said slowly, "but it still seems to me whoever set up that complicated a scheme—if they really did—could have thought of a way out of it, once he calmed down, even if he did panic initially."

"But the whole scheme had gone sky-west and galley-crooked," I argued, "because they got blood and brain tissue splattered all over the back seat of what was supposed to be a clean car. At that point there was no way they could both get clear, and of course with Patrick dead it didn't matter to whoever his partner was whether Patrick got clear or not. So all he could do—X, I mean—was let us follow the trail to the two bodies, and do the best he could to cover his own trail. And so far, at that, he's succeeded."

Harry sat and stared at the table. Then he said, "Deb, you've got a powerful imagination."

That was what Captain Millner would say, if I'd propounded this theory to him. All right, I do have a powerful imagination. It's one of my greatest weaknesses as an investigator—sometimes I reason way ahead of my data—but it's also one of my greatest strengths as an investigator, because I can put one and one and one together with the one we haven't found yet and come up with the four that's there even if I do then have to backtrack to find the missing one.

What was going to be the missing one this time? And was it really a one and not a two or a three? Was my four really a four or was I going to turn out to be wrong?

Somebody else had mentioned a '57 Chevrolet today. Who was it? I had to think before I remembered that it was Captain Millner. I had remembered that Oliver Kelly was dead, I had remembered that he crashed into a bridge abutment on a stormy Christmas Eve, but it was Captain Millner who remembered that he'd been driving a '57 Chevrolet.

Fifty-seven Chevrolets were running through this whole case like a leitmotiv. I wondered—

I wondered a lot of things. I got up and finished drying the dishes, which wasn't necessary—I could have let the dishwasher dry them for me, but I was fidgety—and sat back down again. Harry had gone on into the living room and was now sitting at his radio table saying "CQ, CQ, CQ."

Hal was supposedly doing homework. I say supposedly because I'm not sure how much homework can be done to the tunes of Iron Maiden or whatever that awful group he was listening to was called. I started to scream at him to turn it down, but I changed my mind and went to take a shower instead. After I took the shower then I'd scream at him to turn it down if Harry hadn't done so in the meantime.

I was sitting at my desk making a list of things to do with Aline watching me restlessly. So far, the list included locating Audrey and Roma and talking with them (I considered that a low priority item but Captain Millner didn't seem to agree), finding proof that Susanna French and Susie Kelly were the same person (Dutch was supposedly doing that but I still wanted it on my list), calling the motor vehicle registration people and asking for a printout of all the 1957 Chevrolets still on the road in Texas.

I leaned back to think about 1957 Chevrolets. Collectible. I'd been told they were collectible. Anything that's collectible usually has a club devoted to it. Had Patrick Kelly and X been members of that club? Whether or not they had, certainly they had to have been friends for a very long time, had to have been working together for a reasonably long time, for their individual cars to look so much alike as to give this plan a hope of succeeding. How long had Kelly been rebuilding his—about two and a half years, maybe three years? And he'd been working at French's Chevrolet

Agency almost that whole time, well, up until the last five months anyway. Most likely he'd ordered some of the parts through that agency, some from other Chevrolet agencies in Dallas, Fort Worth. Presumably the other person had done the same, or had Kelly gotten the parts for both cars because he could—maybe—get a discount, at least while he was working for French.

"Deb," Aline asked, "what are you doing?"

"Making lists."

"No, you're not, you're staring off into space. Look, somebody has to go wandering around and picking up those lists of people who've worked at SellAmerica, so I guess I ought to do that. Anything else you want me to do in Dallas and Arlington?"

"Yeah," I said, "go talk to French."

"Look, Deb, I don't know how much like talking that man is going to feel."

"He's not going to feel a bit like talking," I agreed, "but he's got to all the same."

"Okay, what am I supposed to ask him about?" Aline asked wearily.

"Find out if he knows Susanna was married before she married him. Find out whether she was using her previous married name or her maiden name when he met her. Find out if he knows her previous married name, and find out where they got married, and if he knows where she got divorced from Kelly find that out."

"I think one of the postal inspectors already got that."

"Okay, then find out the rest of it anyway. Also, see if he knows about Kelly rebuilding that—"

"Deb, you told me yourself he said he didn't even know Patrick Kelly, so how could he possibly know about—"

"He must have known him by some sort of nickname. I know a big automobile agency has a lot of employees, but all the same he ought to know somebody who worked for him for two years."

"Well—"

"And find out if he knew of anybody else rebuilding a car the same way. You might need to talk with the parts department. And with—"

"With the people he knew that worked there, okay."

"Aline, try to find out without asking whether any of them at all knew he used to be married to French's wife."

"You know it may take me days to do all this."

"Do it as fast as you can anyway."

"Okay, I'm going to sleep at home tonight," Aline said, "instead of in a motel in Fort Worth, and I may wind up having to do some of this talking with people tomorrow. I'll try to get back here by noon tomorrow anyway. What are you going to be doing today?"

"I'm going to break away after a while and go to Patrick's funeral."

"What in the world do you want to do that for? Don't you know it's an exploded theory that murderers always show up at their victim's funeral?"

I shrugged. "This time it might not be. I suspect whoever killed Patrick knows him well enough it would be conspicuous at least to the family and friends for him *not* to show up."

"So the corpse will sit up and begin to bleed and say 'Thou art the Man'—"

"All right, Aline," I said, "laugh if you want to but I still think whoever killed Patrick is going to be at his funeral. Anyway I know his sisters will be, and—"

Aline shrugged. "Have it your way. I'm gone."

It was nearly nine; the funeral was at eleven. I had time to go by one of the local Chevrolet agencies—I picked Carson's because I knew the owner—and ask some questions.

The new car sales floor was officially open, but "Kit" Carson was back in the service area, which of course had been open since six-thirty. Carson had owned this agency nearly fifty years, and he liked to keep his hands in all the pies. When the receptionist called him in to talk to me, he told me he'd been looking at the cars brought in for repair to see how many had been sold by somebody other than him, to use that information in planning his next advertising campaign. "Service is important," he informed me, "and a lot of people will buy their next car on the basis of who gives them the best service."

"I can believe that," I agreed. "I got ahold of a lemon once—it was a used car, because that was all I could afford then—but all the same it made me so mad because I kept having to take it back and take it back because nobody would fix it so it stayed fixed."

"What seemed to be wrong with it?"

"It kept getting a clogged fuel filter, and every time it got clogged the car would hiccup and die and not want to go over twenty miles an hour and act like the transmission was messed up. They kept changing it but every time they changed it it would just clog right back up."

"That's a design problem, then, if they kept changing the filter and it still kept clogging that fast. Or else you were using cheap gas. Were you using cheap gas?"

"Exxon."

"That ought to be all right, then, unless the station was buying some of its gas bootleg. That's a big problem, you know, and the Mafia and all is mixed up in it some places. But I don't know if we're getting any of it here yet."

"I hope not," I said. "We got enough trouble as it is."

We were in the showroom now, bright and comfortable, the new cars highlighted by plants, bright posters, color charts. Some of the salesmen were wandering around looking busy and important. I suppose that if you're a salesman you have to look busy and important even if you aren't really doing anything at all.

"Okay," Carson said, sitting down in his office across the desk from me as if he were about to sell me a car, "tell me the trouble."

"Kit, what is a fifty-seven Chevrolet worth?"

"What kind of condition is it in?"

"Any kind of condition."

"Lord, what a question." He grinned at me, his white mustache making him look more like Colonel Sanders than like the original Kit Carson. "If it's been sitting on the back of a used car lot and nobody's done any work on it since its fifty-thousand mile checkup and it's got two hundred thousand miles on it, maybe a hundred and fifty, two hundred dollars, or maybe more, because people are buying them to—well, let me back up, what kind of fifty-seven Chevrolet are we talking about? Because if it was a hardtop coupe it would be worth quite a little bit of dough even if nobody had done a thing to it, just because it was a good little car and people *are* buying them to restore. But if it's just a plain sedan, probably not over a hundred and fifty, if it's in really bad shape. Let me put it this way—if somebody drove in here this morning with a hardtop coupe that looked like it'd been through a mangle, if it was in restorable condition at all I'd give him five hundred for it at least and maybe more because I'd get it back and then some. That help any?"

"Who would you sell it to?"

"Whoever wanted to buy it, of course. What kind of a question is that?"

"But would you advertise it, or call a collectors' club, or—"

"There is a collectors' club. Is that what you wanted to know? I'd give you the president's name only I forgot it. Bill Conners will know. Sometimes they meet at his agency."

"So I'll call Bill Conners. Now what if it's in perfect shape, looks like it just drove out of the showroom completely equipped with all the options you could get?"

Carson leaned forward in his car. "A hardtop coupe in that kind of shape? You know where I can find one?"

"We've got one in the pound."

"You've got to be kidding."

"I'm not kidding. We've got one in the pound. We need to find out who it belongs to, because it's mixed up in a killing." Actually we knew who it belonged to, Patrick Kelly. It was the burned one we needed to trace. But I didn't want to get into that, and Carson wouldn't know the difference.

"That Kelly thing? Kelly had one of his own, you know. But I thought the paper said it was burned."

"It was. This looks just like Kelly's, though. We think the owner of this car is the person who burned Kelly's car."

"Just like Kelly's, exactly? That makes me sick, somebody burning that car."

There it was again, the car mentioned over the three people dead. There certainly must be something I couldn't understand about the 1957 Chevrolet. "As far as we can tell, yes, exactly like Kelly's."

"Honey, I'd give thirty thousand dollars for it without blinking, because I know I'd get it back with interest."

"That's more than my first house cost."

"That's more than most people's first house cost, unless they're under thirty. It was a good running car. It was a good-looking car. It still is. Only then it was transportation and now it's a toy. Most often a rich man's toy, but not always. You think it'll go on the market? Maybe go up for auction, if you don't find the owner?"

"It won't go for auction. We've got to find the owner. I told you, he's mixed up in a killing."

"Mixed up how?" Carson grinned. "I guess you can't tell me that, can you?"

"Really I can't. Do you know of another one like Kelly's?"

"You mean just like? Same color and everything?"

"Just like."

"Uh-uh. That dark forest green, it wasn't real popular. Most popular colors were a pretty sky blue and that candy apple red. I guess the candy apple red was the best selling, but we sold a lot of the blue and more'n a few of the pink. I don't think I sold more than eight or ten of the green, but lordy, I don't keep that kind of records. I'm going on memory, and you know how many years ago that's been?"

"More than I want to remember. The first one I ever saw belonged to my junior high history teacher." Now why did I remember that? I don't remember cars. It must have been memorable, to have stuck with me like that. "You've never seen another dark green?"

"I didn't say that. I just told you I sold—"

"I mean recently. Say, in the last five months or so."

"Not that I can recall. The green tended to fade, you know. A lot of them were repainted."

Paint. There's always paint. If you can paint over green, you can paint green over another color just as easily. "Do you remember any of the people who own cars like his but other colors?"

Carson closed his eyes. "Honey, how do you 'spect me to remember that? I'm seventy-five years old."

I hate being called honey by anybody, and especially by casual acquaintances, but I wanted information more than I wanted to object. "Okay, suppose I had one and I was working on restoring it, would I be able to get parts through your parts department?"

"You could, but you'd be a damn fool if you did."

"Explain?"

"There are catalogs, specialty catalogs, for people into that sort of thing. They get the parts wholesale and sell them just a little above wholesale. We sell 'em retail. And I'm damned if I'm going to tell you what the markup is on car parts. You might want to buy some from me someday."

"If I talk to your parts department will they be able to tell me if somebody's been ordering parts for a fifty-seven Chevrolet?"

"They might can. I'll take you around there."

But—as Kit Carson had predicted—nobody in the parts department could remember anybody ordering any 1957 parts. Wilma Fox, parts manager, said she thought she'd remember an order like that even if she didn't remember who'd placed it. She said she'd have somebody look through invoices, if I really needed her to, but five months' worth of invoices, and they'd have to do it around current work—

I told her not to worry about it for now. It probably wasn't worth the trouble.

"Well, there has been one," Wilma added, "but I guess you know about that one."

"Who's that? And why would I know?"

"Well, because it's Billy Jack Turner, and I know you must've talked with Lantana used to be Kelly, and Billy Jack's her husband."

Which told me Wilma Fox was local from the same part of town I was local from. "No, I didn't know that. I mean I know Billy Jack, sure, but I didn't know he had—that I did not know. Thank you, Wilma."

Billy Jack. I'd already been planning to go talk again with Lantana this afternoon, to try to find out where Roma and Audrey had taken themselves to, but this made it even more urgent. If Billy Jack had a 1957 Chevrolet—or even more, if Billy Jack *didn't* have a 1957 Chevrolet I could look at—

But how could Billy Jack have spent the time he'd have to have spent on this crime, without Lantana knowing about it? And I would swear that Lantana hadn't known.

It wouldn't make sense to try to talk to Billy Jack now. He'd be getting ready to go to a funeral. Knowing the old southern conventionality of the Kellys, which probably extended to the Kelly in-laws, he'd probably be at the funeral home or over at the church already.

The church. Shiloh Baptist Church. That little white asbestos-siding building. The Kellys were so closely linked to that church—they'd all been baptized there, they'd all gone to church there, Sunday school and vacation Bible school and Wednesday night prayer meeting and Sunday night services and autumn revivals in tents in front of the building, and you name it they'd been to it, and Patrick Kelly had shot Sonny Kelly in front of it but Sonny had been buried from inside it all the same.

And somewhere near that old church building Rick Mossberg and his daughter Candy were—alive or dead.

More likely dead, because if they were alive there was no reason they should have been missing for five days now. Five days in the fall, and there had been rain, and the nights were beginning to turn a little cool.

Harry had been in the air but he wouldn't be now, because he'd told me at breakfast this morning, looking a little shamefaced about it, that he intended to go to the funeral too. So I'd meet him there, I guessed.

I hadn't worn my usual slacks suit today; I'd worn a skirted suit—always a suit, even in maternity clothes, with a jacket to hide my shoulder holster, but usually it was a pants suit. As long as I didn't take my jacket off I'd look, all day long, like somebody approved by Mr. Molloy of *Dress for Success* fame. That, for me, is rare. But in a navy blue skirted suit I could go to a southern funeral and look acceptable, although a frilly blue dress with a white Peter Pan collar would of course be far preferable. You cannot wear a shoulder holster with a frilly blue dress with a white Peter Pan collar. And I'd really be in trouble if I had to chase anybody in these darned awful high-heeled shoes. I hate high-heeled shoes at the best of times, and I was now finding that they threw me badly off balance.

The church sits on a hill. It's old, probably old enough to rate a historical marker if anybody cared enough to give it one, and the asbestos siding is white. The porch is painted gray, that durable out-of-doors gray paint that is used for barns in Texas far more often than red is. The two little rooms off the front foyer, one on each side, are normally used for Sunday school, but they can be opened up to provide more seating for large weddings and funerals.

They weren't going to be needed today.

The floor was pine varnished to look like hardwood,

with the varnish almost worn off and soft gray splinters wearing through in spots. The pews were brown-painted wood with no cushions. I joined Harry near the back, not hoping to be unnoticed—we would certainly be noticed—but because I didn't want to intrude on the real sorrow of Lantana and anybody else who might happen to be seriously mourning the death of Patrick Kelly.

I'd felt an impostor as I signed the guest register in the small entrance hall that was called foyer only by courtesy. And yet it wasn't all fake; I wasn't here just as a police officer. I had known the Kellys all my life; my mother and Patrick's mother had been friends (and yes, there *was* my mother, sitting primly in the fourth row). As a law enforcement officer, I strongly objected to Patrick Kelly's conduct past and present, and yet, if I had known when Patrick came back to Fort Worth, if he'd stayed out of trouble and I'd met him one day on the street I wouldn't have had anything but a greeting for him. I still remembered, so well, the shock that had whirled around our little corner of the city when Patrick shot Sonny—Patrick had been popular, but then, so had Sonny.

There weren't many people there I didn't recognize. The pastor—I'd called him Brother Green when I was a child—didn't seem to have changed much, except to grow imperceptibly older.

After a long prayer, there was a congregational sing of "Shall We Gather at the River." Then the funeral sermon began, with a reading of First Thessalonians 4:13. "But I would not have you to be ignorant, brethren, concerning them which are asleep, that ye sorrow not, even as others which have no hope." That was the text Brother Green always used for a funeral sermon; this time, it seemed woefully inappropriate. He intoned something about "them also which sleep in Jesus." Could a man who had shot and killed his brother, and later killed a child by shutting her up in the trunk of a car, be said to "sleep in Jesus"? I didn't think so. I shut my ears off and looked around.

The once large Kelly family was sadly decimated. There were Lantana and Billy Jack and their three anemic-looking children. There was Audrey, so changed I almost couldn't recognize her. There was Roma. She had a rather substantial-looking man sitting with her, and two children, a boy about twelve and a girl about fourteen. Two or three elderly aunts I recognized by feature but not by name. A few old school teachers. A few old men, probably there out of respect to the memory of Kelly's parents. A few old women who went to all the funerals. Three retired Fort Worth policemen, apparently remembering Patrick Kelly as an ex-cop and deliberately choosing to forget his more recent history.

Beside my mother was Sister Dakle, my old Sunday school teacher and probably Patrick's too, because she'd been teaching Sunday school over sixty years. I'd never known her to miss a funeral. Beside her was Sister Green, the pastor's wife. She never missed funerals either, although she certainly could have recited the sermon any time for the last thirty years, and in fact right now she looked as if she were about to go to sleep.

There were a few other men, all of them looking as if they did a lot of manual labor, all of them looking distinctly uncomfortable in suits, all of them flanked by women mostly neatly dressed in frilly dark blue dresses.

The sermon finally ended. Another hymn and another long prayer followed, and everybody filed out to the cars. There weren't enough friends and relatives of

Patrick Kelly to be pallbearers, and the men from the funeral home took care of that task.

"Do you think we ought to go to the graveside?" I asked Harry.

Harry shrugged. "We're here, we might as well go on. But I'd forgotten how much I hate funerals." We headed for our own car.

"At least this one wasn't open casket." I hate open casket funerals even more than Harry hates funerals.

"From what you tell me, it couldn't be."

"Morticians do wonderful things with makeup," I said gloomily. "I've seen open caskets following car wrecks so messed up that you couldn't tell who was who."

"Blech," Harry said. "If you have an open casket for me I swear I'll come back and haunt you." He turned the car into the ceremonial procession, switching his headlights on. "We'll come back for your police car later," he added.

And had Patrick Kelly's killer been there in the church? I couldn't tell. Nearly everybody looked uncomfortable. Nobody looked especially guilty.

But somehow I had a hunch somebody in there was guilty, if I just had some way to know who.

What does it profit a man if he gain the whole world and lose his soul?

Somebody had two hundred and fifty thousand dollars that he couldn't even spend, because if he started to spend it he'd have to explain where it came from, and no matter what story he came up with somebody—sometime—was going to begin to wonder.

And begin to suspect.

· 9 ·

"And so much for your plan of going to the funeral," Captain Millner said, after one look at my face. "Did you see anybody there you didn't expect to see?"

"No," I admitted, "but the thing is, it's real likely the person we're looking for *is* somebody we'd expect to see at Patrick Kelly's funeral."

"What did you see there? Farmers? Old men? You really think one of them was a murderer?"

"Patrick Kelly looked like a farmer, and he was a murderer."

"True," Millner admitted. "But you're not talking about somebody cutting loose with a thirty-eight in the middle of the street, now. You're talking about some sort of supercrook with a lot of planning ability. Deb, I'm not calling farmers stupid. They aren't. They can't be, with all the things they have to know. But I am saying there's a lot of difference between knowing how to plant and fertilize and harvest and fix the tractor, and knowing how to plan a major crime and have some kind of hope of getting away with it. It's a totally different type of knowledge, and you know that as well as I do."

I shrugged. "All the same, Billy Jack Turner was buying parts for a 1957 Chevrolet."

"When did you find that out?"

"This morning. Before the funeral."

"So go talk with Billy Jack Turner again—uh-oh. We got company."

I turned, and headed quickly toward Deborah Mossberg. "Mrs. Mossberg, what's—"

"Have they found my baby yet?" she demanded. "That's all. Have they found my baby yet?"

"They're still looking, Mrs. Mossberg," I said, in my most soothing tone. This wasn't the overdressed, would-be sophisticated cocktail waitress I'd met the first day; Deborah Mossberg, sans makeup, sans elaborate hairdo, sans seductive clothing, was a young, slightly pretty woman who was very upset and very worried. She wasn't drinking, but she didn't seem to have been eating, either, and I steered her to a chair before she fell over. She leaned over the desk, crying.

"But why can't they find them? And why didn't they come out of the woods anyway? Rick wouldn't get lost! Rick knows the woods, he knows—"

"We don't know why they didn't come out. We can't know that until they're located."

"But do you think they're all right?" It was an anguished wail, and Dutch, who'd just come in with a paper cup of Coke in his hand, looked startled and then handed it to the woman.

She drank it mechanically, which gave me a little bit

of a breather while I thought about what to say. A soothing lie, as convenient as it might be, would be a lie, and I was pretty sure Deborah would spot it as a lie. "I wish I could answer you, but we just don't know, not yet."

"It was all my fault—"

Here we go, I thought resignedly; most likely Roma and Audrey would have gone home by the time I could disentangle myself from this.

I didn't want to stand here and listen to Deborah Mossberg lay a guilt trip on herself, but somebody had to listen to Deborah Mossberg, and although the case now officially belonged to Dutch, I was better equipped than Dutch to listen to a hysterical young woman. "Deborah," I said in the most soothing tones I could muster, "you know all this crying really isn't going to help anything. I know it's awful to just have to sit and wait, but we've got a lot of people out looking for them—my husband is out looking from the air, in a helicopter— and they're bound to turn up."

"Yeah," Deborah sobbed, "yeah, sure they will, only will they be alive? It was all my fault—"

Let her get it off her chest, I thought. Then maybe she'd stop crying. "How could it possibly be your fault?"

"I looked—" heaving sobs—"at the paper. At the want ads. Sunday. And Monday. And yesterday. Rick was right. He really couldn't get a job. See, he works real hard, nobody works harder than Rick, but there's just so many things he can do. Do you know what they're hiring people to do?"

"Uh-uh. What?"

"They want clerk typists. And they want insurance salesmen. And they want people to sell cars. And they want computer programmers. Rick can't do any of that! Rick works with his hands."

"Okay."

"But—" Another heaving sob. "I didn't want to believe him. Because—because—" Now her words were coming out in a rush. "I grew up in a house with eight children and only one bedroom and no bathroom at all, we used an outdoor toilet—I'll bet you didn't know anybody really still did that, did you—but we did. We didn't have anything—we were so poor, and we were on welfare, and we dressed in old rags other people gave us, and I had to clean tables in the school lunchroom to get any lunch, and I said when I grew up I'd never, never, never, never be poor again—and we didn't have very much money when Rick was in the army, we weren't starving, I don't mean that, we had enough to eat and a place to live and the medical benefits and all that, but it was just enough and not anything to spare, to have fun with, to buy pretty clothes with, and then when Rick got out of the army and he went to work for that drilling place, Deb, he was making twenty-one dollars an hour! And that's a lot of money and it was *wonderful* and even when he got cut back to four days a week it was still more money than either of us had ever seen, and I could buy Candy all the pretty clothes I always wanted when I was a kid and never could get, and we had meat on the table at every meal if we wanted to, and then he got laid off. And I didn't ever want to be poor again and I was so scared and he kept going out looking for a job and coming home and saying he couldn't find one and then the supplemental unemployment ran out and I thought he just wasn't trying, I thought he just didn't want to have a job anymore like my daddy, because my daddy never would have a job, he just lay up on the porch swing and drank up all the welfare money and we grew corn and collards to eat and I thought Rick was going to start being like that and so I thought I would find a job and I did, I got that job at the Rig and it paid good and I could still get Candy pretty clothes, and milk, but Rick got mad and he said that was a crummy place for me to work and it was just about half a step above being a whore and it wasn't, it wasn't, I wouldn't—"

"Of course you wouldn't," I murmured. Rick's suggestion was quite uncalled-for; a cocktail waitress runs her feet off.

"But he got mad and he wanted to go to Dallas and I was scared because how did *I* know he'd find a job in Dallas, or me either one, and he wanted us to sleep in the truck while he was hunting a job, and you can't take care of a baby living in a truck, and he said Candy isn't a baby and I said yes she is, a six-year-old is still a baby, and as long as I had that job I could keep the house and I could buy nice things for Candy and I was just a waitress, that's all, and Rick didn't have no call to get so mad—"

"Of course he didn't."

"And I said Rick could go to Dallas by himself and he said he was scared if he did I wouldn't take care of Candy and I don't need nobody to tell me how to take care of my baby and I got mad back and I said if he didn't like my job he could just get out because he wasn't doing nothing anyway, only he really was and that was a crummy thing for me to say because when I was looking after the house and Candy I was busy all the time so why was it when Rick was looking after the house and Candy why did I think he wasn't doing nothing? He was doing just as much as I was when I was—"

By now she'd almost quit crying. Thank goodness, I thought. "Some people just don't handle role reversal very well."

"What's role reversal?"

"It's when people wind up doing what we think of as each other's jobs in life."

"Oh. Well, I guess Rick and me just don't handle role reversals very well. Because he was mad because I was earning the living and he was staying at home and I was mad because he was staying at home and I was earning the living so I told him to get out so he got out and then I said he couldn't see Candy and that was really crummy of me, wasn't it?"

"I'm afraid it was."

"Because he and Candy always had a lot of fun together and maybe I was jealous, do you suppose?"

"Maybe so."

"And he wanted to go back in the army and I said I wouldn't move away from my mom anymore so if he joined the army I'd stay home. And he said that's no kind of marriage at all. And I said no kind of marriage is what we've got, and I told him to get out, and he said he'd already got out what else did I want and I said I wanted a divorce. Deb, if he gets back all right and Candy's all right I promise I won't get mad anymore."

"All people get mad. Maybe what you'd better promise is that when you're mad you'll think before you start yelling."

"All right, then I'll promise that, because I love my baby and I really love Rick and I want that divorce to go away and I want another baby even if Rick is in the army and I don't care where we live and I *hate* that awful job, half those oil men have fourteen hands apiece you know what I mean, and I keep telling them I don't want none of that I just want to go home to my baby and they laugh and think that's funny and then Carol gets better tips than I do because when they grab

· 181 ·

her she giggles but I need those tips a lot more than Carol does, and—and—" She was sobbing again. "It's all my fault because if I hadn't said he couldn't see Candy then I bet they wouldn't have gone off in the woods like that."

"I thought you told me they like to camp."

"Well, they do, but—"

"Then I'll bet they just went camping and maybe had some kind of trouble and couldn't get out as fast as they expected to."

"They never did before. Isn't there anything I can do to help find them?"

Obviously there was not. The last thing in the world the search party needed was a distraught woman tramping around in the woods getting herself lost too. I thought fast. "What church do you go to?"

Another sob. "C-Catholic."

"Is Rick Catholic too?"

"Uh-huh. And the priest was really mad at us when—"

"Well, what I think you should do now is go tell the priest exactly what you told me," I said, "and see if he can make any suggestions. And you might—" I searched my brain for what little I knew about Catholicism—"you might make a novena."

The sobbing died down. "Yeah, I could do that. But what if I make a novena and then they still aren't back?"

"I kind of think they will be." Dead or alive, I thought. If they're in the area at all we should have found them—dead or alive—long before that special nine-day prayer vigil is over.

"You really think I ought to talk to my priest?"

"I think you should. You'd probably feel a lot better, and he might have some suggestions I wouldn't."

"Okay." Deborah got a Kleenex out of her purse and paused, startled, at the one-way mirror that allowed room-to-room lineups without the viewer being visible to the prisoners. Not suspecting it was anything other than a mirror, she leaned over and examined her face. "I look awful. I better do something about that. Rick gets so mad when I look awful."

"Go on and talk with your priest," I advised, "and worry later about how you look."

"I'll do that. Yeah, I'll do that. Thank you. You'll let me know, won't you, when—when—"

"Somebody will get in touch with you at once," I promised, and watched as Deborah, still sobbing slightly, left. Then I turned, reached for my car keys, and headed out the door after her.

Lantana Turner looked at me with something close to hostility. "Why can't you people leave us alone?" she asked. "My brother was just buried. Why do you have to bother us now?" She set her purse on the table and sat down, wobbling just a little as she crossed the room in unaccustomed high-heel shoes.

"I was at the funeral," I said, "and I know this is a really bad time for you. But we've had a little more evidence turn up—" that wasn't exactly a lie, I thought— "and we think somebody set Patrick up."

"You mean he didn't do it?"

"Oh, he did it. But we think it's possible that somebody conned him into something that wasn't supposed to go near as far as it did, and then killed him. We have to find out who that someone is. And to do that I need to talk with you some more."

"Look, Deb, I done already told you all I know."

"Lantana, I don't think for a second there's anything you haven't told me, if you have any reason to think it

matters. I just keep thinking there's something somebody hasn't told me because they don't think it matters
at all, and that might be what I need."

Lantana shrugged. "You want some tea?"

"I've gotten where I can't drink tea," I said. "Maybe
some plain water?"

"I never did get where I couldn't drink tea," Lantana
said. "But boy, coffee sure did smell horrible." She got
me a glass of water, walking around Billy Jack. He still
hadn't spoken at all; he sat unsmiling backward on a
chair, his chin on his hands on the back of the chair,
staring at me. Even in the rusty-looking black suit he
couldn't possibly wear often, he still had ground-in oil
in the creases of his knuckles.

"Okay, you're here, you might as well stay, I guess,"
Lantana added. "Right, Billy Jack?"

Billy Jack made an incoherent noise that might, or
might not, have been assent. I decided to take it as assent anyway.

"The first thing I need to know is, where can I locate
Audrey and Roma to talk to? I want to talk with every-
body in the family, because there's always the chance
Patrick might have said something to somebody—"

"If Patrick had told Audrey or Roma he was getting
mixed up with something like that," Lantana interrupted, "they'd have done the same thing I would've.
They'd have kicked his butt good."

"I realize that, Lantana. I've been telling everybody
that you're all good, church-going people. But I am just
about sure he was killed by somebody he knew, and he
might have mentioned this person to one of them.
What I'm trying to say, and I guess I'm not making a
very good job of it, is, he could have said something
that wouldn't mean anything to you but it would mean
a lot to us."

"Oh. Okay. Well, Audrey is living in Garland."

"Garland? That helps; that's not very far away." Garland is on the other side of Dallas. "What's her married name?"

"Well, she's a widow."

"Yeah?" I said, wondering what that had to do with her name.

"She was married to a Joe Hickson and he died a couple of years back. Lung cancer. Smoked from the time he was ten years old. My daddy would've whupped my ass if I'd tried that. But anyway she's working in a day care center in Garland. I can give you her phone number." She turned, to drag an address book off a nearby shelf.

"Thanks, that would help a lot. Can you get Roma's at the same time?"

"Yeah, I can, but you might as well just look in the phone book for Roma."

"I thought Roma moved away."

"She did. She moved down to Houston. But then she moved back. Carl—that's her husband, Carl Gilbert— he just wasn't making a living down there and so they moved back to Fort Worth a couple of years back. He sells insurance, so you can bet he's listed in the phone book."

"Yeah, I remember Carl, but I didn't know they'd moved back. Thanks a lot. One more question and then I'll get out of your way. Patrick had a nineteen fifty-seven Chevrolet hardtop coupe, real nice. He had a friend that had one too, and I need to know who that was."

"Lady, I've got one," Billy Jack said. His voice was unexpectedly deep. "You want to see it?"

"I sure would like to."

"Then come on."

Billy Jack disentangled himself from the chair and led me out the back door, a short man walking slightly bowlegged. We walked through the well-kept-up backyard of the trailer, through a small gate, onto a dirt track that led through the trailer court, and into a long shed at the back, overgrown with some kind of vine.

"There 'tis," Billy Jack said proudly. "I've wanted one for years, ever since Patrick and Oliver got theirs. I tried to get Patrick to sell me his, while he was in prison, but he said nothing doing. Last year I finally found this one sitting at the back of a used car lot in Hughes Springs, with all four tires flat and a cracked block, and I talked the dude into letting me tow it off for a hundred and fifty dollars. It's got a long way to go before it looks as good as Patrick's, but hell, it's something to do when I ain't got nothing else to do."

The Chevrolet—yet another hardtop coupe—was candy apple red. And it was in pieces; the engine block was sitting in a corner of the garage with weeds growing through it; one fender was off, and all four tires were missing.

"You got a lot of work ahead of you," I said, "but it's going to be worth it."

"You better believe it's going to be worth it." Billy Jack grinned proudly at the wreckage. "You won't believe how good this baby is going to look and run five years from now."

"It'll really be a lot of work, I guess."

"But this wasn't the one you want, right?"

"Right. The one I want looked just like Patrick's, same color and everything. In perfect condition. You seen it?"

"Oh, lady, I don't know. Patrick's was the only green one I can think of. Green really wasn't a very good color for these babies, there was a nice sky blue, and this here red like I've got—"

That was information I already had.

Billy Jack added, "You might ask Carl. He's my brother-in-law, Roma's husband, that you was asking about, and he drove Patrick's a lot. If there was another one around he might know about it. He and Patrick got along pretty good."

"You and Patrick didn't?"

Billy Jack chuckled. "Lady, I feel just a little nervous around somebody that pulled out a gun and shot his brother. Me and Lantana, we was married by then—"

I didn't remember that. Lantana couldn't have been over sixteen. But I did remember she'd finally dropped out of school.

"I knew Susie," Billy Jack was continuing. "She wasn't bad, she was just a little bit frisky, and she wouldn't have really cheated on Patrick. She and Sonny was just a-whispering a little. If Lantana'd a-done that I'd whup her ass, that's all, but Patrick done pulled out a gun and shot Sonny cold dead, and Sonny didn't have no harm in him. He was as wuthless as any man the good Lord ever put on this earth, but he was a good ol' boy. And if Patrick got mad and shot Sonny how do I know Patrick won't get mad at me someday? No. I didn't quarrel with Patrick, but I sure didn't look to go visit him."

"I hear you," I agreed. "Well, they say every big family's got one. I guess it's been rough on Lantana."

"You can say that again. Patrick was her big brother, and I guess girls don't never get over that 'big brother can't do no wrong' feeling. She knows it with her head but her stomach sure as hell don't know it."

"Okay. I appreciate talking with you, Billy Jack. Sorry it had to be this kind of circumstance."

"Sure. Come on over whenever you want to. Lantana likes to see old friends."

I went to my office and made more lists.

Call Bill Conners and ask about the collectors' club, whatever its name was.

Call Susan.

Then I had to stop and think. Things had been happening so fast that I couldn't remember whether I had told Susan about the second green car or not. That might make a certain amount of difference in the conclusions she reached. And I hadn't told her. I couldn't possibly have told her, because I hadn't talked with Susan since before we found it.

Or at least, before *I* knew about it. I indulged in a moment's silent detestation of Danny Shea, and then I called Susan.

Susan was with a patient and could not be disturbed. I left a message, which I hope was coherent, about the second dark green 1957 Chevrolet, and then I called Bill Conners at Conners Chevrolets. Bill Conners was not quite as hard to get to talk with as the president of the United States might be.

As I was waiting on hold—for the third time in the same telephone call—I recalled once seeing a telephone number scrawled on a wall. It was an overseas England telephone number, complete with all dialing codes, numbers, and extensions, and it purported to be the private telephone number of the queen of England. I never called it to see whether it really was; I wonder how many people did. I wonder if it was. Probably not. And I was beginning to wonder, with just as much exasperation or maybe a little more, since I didn't really need to talk with anybody in England, whether I was ever really going to get to talk with Bill Conners at all.

But just as I was wondering that a hearty used-car-salesman voice came on the line. "Conners here."

I introduced myself, feeling unaccountably tired of the sound of my own voice saying my own name, and asked about collectors' clubs.

Well, there was one, Conners allowed, but it was mainly in Dallas. They had this nice display at the car show every year, and it was a shame I'd just missed it.

I agreed that it was a shame I'd just missed it, and asked who I could talk with.

Conners gave me a name and, after some hesitation that seemed to involve scratching around on his desk, a telephone number.

Of course I called it. Of course there was no answer. Conners had told me he couldn't give me the business phone number of the person because he didn't know it, sorry. And of course that would be the phone number to reach the person, at this time on a weekday.

I'd call it again on my own time, I supposed, and tried again to call Susan.

Susan was still with a patient and could not be disturbed.

Rats, I thought, and called the DMV to ask about getting a printout.

Surprise, surprise, not foiled again. The DMV said it would get me a printout and if I wanted to go to the closest highway patrol station they'd have it ready for me. When could I go to pick it up, I asked, and the nice voice at the other end said just about any old time I wanted to, if I wanted to come to where he was and get it, because he sure did like the sound of my voice.

Surprise, surprise, nice baritone voice, I'm forty-two, married, and pregnant. But I'll be glad to come out and pick up the printout.

The voice laughed, told me his name was Mark Hudson and it didn't hurt to try, he'd met an awful lot of nice females that way.

I drove out to the highway patrol station, picked up the printout, and decided to keep on going. I wasn't far from Braun Clinic; since I couldn't seem to catch Susan free on the telephone, I'd just go out and camp in her waiting room and sooner or later she'd make time to see me.

I didn't know I was going to go to sleep in her waiting room. But it was just as well. It was a while before she was free.

Susan's office is like her: both professional and non- (not un-) professional. It has bookshelves lined with books and a desk littered with assorted doodads for nervous people—patients, relatives of patients, and anyone else who strays into the domain of a mental hospital— to fidget with. Susan likes to fidget with them too.

And with everything else. Susan is a very fidgety person.

"It's a maxim, not necessarily a truism, that there are no real accidents," she told me, carefully lining up her desk pad, three pens, and several large paper clips in a neat, straight row like cars on a railroad train. "Well, of course it isn't true. There are real accidents, though they're a lot rarer than the general public supposes. But an accident-prone person is almost certainly a person who on at least some level wants to have accidents."

"Why would anybody want to have accidents?"

"They get something out of it. Time off from a hated

job, sympathy and attention from family, any number of possible rewards. It's like my hair."

"What about your hair?"

Susan methodically began to remove the bobby pins insecurely anchoring one straggling braid. "I'm like the White Queen. I address it and address it but it never does any good. But subconsciously I must *like* my hair to keep falling down—" she was now reattaching the bobby pins and speaking through her teeth around the ones she was holding in her mouth—"so that I'll have something to fool with, because obviously, if I didn't like it, why, I'd just get it all cut off!" Triumphantly she reinserted the last bobby pins and the braid at once fell down. "See what I mean?" she asked, detaching bobby pins again.

"Yeah. It's like Harry changing diapers. He didn't want to, so every time he changed one he changed it so loosely that as soon as the baby stood up the diaper fell off. But I'm not sure what that has to do with this case."

"That poor child—Helen French—accidentally died. They didn't mean to kill her, they just shut her up in the trunk a little while to keep her quiet and maybe out of sight until they got away from the school; they didn't know she had asthma. Patrick Kelly accidentally died; his friend was just a little careless with a shotgun, he didn't know it was going to go off . . . see what I mean?"

"I think I do," I said slowly. "They knew what the child looked like. He knew she was the only person in her school who went home for lunch. So—"

"So he *did* know she had asthma," Susan finished for me. "Almost certainly he did know. He just let himself forget, and selective forgetting is almost always in some way deliberate."

"You're saying he killed Helen French and Patrick Kelly deliberately, even though their deaths thoroughly messed up his plans?"

"He undoubtedly believes, and will believe until his dying day, that their deaths were accidents. Just as he undoubtedly believes it's been accidents or inexplicable fits of nature or vagaries of the economic cycle that have stymied every other plan he's made in his life. So—you're looking for a man who is accident-prone, who is chronically unfortunate, who is chronically unsuccessful."

"Okay," I said.

"By unsuccessful," Susan went on, "I don't mean just unsuccessful economically. Some people are quite unsuccessful economically and massively successful in other spheres. But he'll be unsuccessful at anything. His interpersonal relationships will turn sour. His home life will always be bad. If he has a garden he forgets to water it—there's that forgetting again. He forgets to change the oil in his car and can't figure out why his engine fails. He forgets to go to his children's events at school. He forgets his anniversary and can't figure out why his wife gets mad at him."

"But subconsciously he wants the car to fail and his children to be disappointed and his wife to be mad at him?"

"Exactly. And that's not all. From what you tell me about the case, he was deliberately imitating Patrick. He almost certainly got his dark green fifty-seven Chevrolet—an unpopular color, mind you—well after Patrick got his. He had to search to find a car like Patrick's. So almost certainly he was identifying with Patrick."

"He was identifying with Patrick and he killed Patrick."

"Exactly. He identified with Patrick and he killed Patrick. Who else did he kill that we know of? He killed Helen French. And who was Helen French? A very sickly child. So it is quite likely that he also identified with Helen French and sees—saw—himself as a sickly child."

"So what does that give us?" I reviewed. "Somebody careless, accident-prone, unsuccessful. If he identifies with Patrick, he's probably got severe marital problems—"

"Which he more than likely created," Susan interposed. "It does not necessarily follow that because he identifies with Patrick he's got an unfaithful wife."

"For that matter we don't even know for sure that Patrick did," I pointed out.

"No, but I can assure you *he* believes Patrick's wife was unfaithful," Susan said.

"He's going to be suicidal," I said. "When we catch him we're going to have to put a suicide watch on him."

Susan nodded, looking pleased. "Yes, there's a lot of self-hatred there. Most likely self-hatred disguised as self-pity, self-solicitude, and I suspect that stems partly from a sickly childhood."

"But not all sick children—"

"No. Not all sick children fall into this trap. But some do. There were undoubtedly other problems than health. I would guess that he hated himself—was made to hate himself—from the very first. What else? Well, he's almost certainly married, he almost certainly has children. If they're robust he overtly despises them for being what he's not, if they're sickly too he covertly despises them for being like him when he doesn't like himself and so doesn't let anybody like him."

"That's a good clear picture," I said. "But there's just one problem."

"What's that?"

"It doesn't fit anybody in this case."

"That's because you haven't gotten to him yet," Susan said confidently. "But you will. You will. And when you find him, I think you'll recognize him right off."

"I will?"

"It's going to be somebody who's known Patrick Kelly for a long, long time. It's going to be somebody who knew Susie Kelly."

"Are you saying she was right that it was because of her?"

"Not in the way she meant it," Susan said. "She was scapegoating herself. But somebody else was scapegoating her too. And that's the person you're looking for."

· 10 ·

Nothing really new had turned up at the Thursday morning briefing session. I was waiting at my desk because Neal Ryan had called to say he was coming to bring me a list from the Department of Public Safety. I wasn't sure what that list could be; the only list I could remember asking for was the one I already had, about the 1957 Chevrolets still on the road. But I had by now asked for so many lists from so many people that I was a little hazy as to who was supposed to be bringing me what.

Meanwhile, of course, I was cleaning out my in-basket, which as usual had somehow filled itself to the brim and overflowed in my absence. I think that every time I am out of the office everybody else empties their in-basket into mine. I was sure that some of these memos I had already read two or three times.

But I conscientiously initialed each one in the upper

left corner to show that I had seen it, and then dumped them into Dutch's in-basket.

Obviously Dutch was not there to defend his territory.

Neal Ryan slouched in; as usual, there was nothing about him that fitted the traditional definition of the word *Ranger* except his hand-tooled leather boots. "I've got you that list," he said, and dumped it unceremoniously in front of me. "Need anything else?"

"Not that I know of," I said, looking with some dismay at a printout that appeared to be identical to the one I had rushed out yesterday afternoon to obtain from the DMV.

"Well, Castillo's asked for it too and I can't get it twice, so give it to him when you're through with it, would you?"

"Actually I—uh—can pass it on to him now," I said. "How so?"

I explained, and Neal shrugged. "Then I'll take it on over to him myself."

While I was waiting for Aline, who wasn't really due until around noon, I figured I might as well have a look at the printout myself. I'd never have guessed this many 1957 Chevrolets would still be on the road in Texas. And I'd kind of expected the list to be alphabetized by owner's name. It wasn't. It was in alphanumeric order by license plate number.

That was going to be a whole lot of fun to check. And I'd have to contact every person on the list if I didn't come up with another way of checking it all, because there was nothing on the list to indicate the color of the cars, and any name on the list conceivably *could* be the owner of the car now in our pound. Some were more likely than others, of course—I couldn't see Sister Mary

Francis, the Rectory, as having participated in a kidnap—but none could be totally ruled out. Sister Mary Francis's car could have been stolen.

I began leafing through the list, marking in red all those close enough to the Dallas–Fort Worth metroplex area to have known Patrick Kelly. But that wasn't really valid. The person didn't have to have come across him in Dallas or Fort Worth. The crime could have been in the planning stages for a long time. It could have been somebody Patrick met in prison.

Susan didn't think so. Susan thought it was somebody Patrick knew before he ever went to prison. Susan is a fine psychiatrist. But a theory is still a theory.

Captain Millner had taken off somewhere, I didn't know where. This Thursday morning there weren't many detectives scheduled on duty; Thursday tends to be the very quietest day of the week in terms of crime, and watch bills usually reflect that. And of the people who were technically on duty, I didn't know where any were. Except for the secretaries' typewriters—excuse me, computer terminals—clicking away, I could have been alone on this floor of the police station.

That was fine with me, as long as the room stayed quiet. I managed to spend the next two hours dictating reports and follow-up reports, all of which were somewhat overdue, and I was just about to leave for lunch when Aline wandered in. "I went to both SellAmerica offices," she announced without preamble, "and I got the lists of people who were working there when the jackets were given out. One is a hundred and sixty-two names long and the other isn't so bad, it's only seventy-three names long."

"Goodie goodie gumdrop," I said. "I got the list from

the DMV yesterday, but that's about all I've gotten done. That and reports."

"Ah, yes, reports. I think I owe about fifty by now."

"Is your list alphabetized?"

"Surely you jest."

"I was afraid of that. This one's not either. Let's go to lunch first and then come back and start comparing lists."

"What are we comparing lists for?" Aline asked.

I thought that was sort of obvious. Maybe it wasn't. "Because our suspect almost surely owns a 1957 Chevrolet—if he'd stolen one it would surely have been reported by now—and we have substantial reason to believe that our suspect very likely had at some time in the past, probably when the jackets were being given out, worked at SellAmerica. So if we can find somebody who's on both lists—"

"That makes sense."

Lunch was going to be a fast hamburger. It was all we had time for.

When I got back into the office, I had a message to call Harry. At home. Why at home, I wondered. He was—I thought—out in the helicopter looking for Rick and Candy Mossberg.

He had been. And he'd found them.

They were camped beside a small stream, under a large live oak tree which had completely blocked them from being seen from the air until he'd come in from just the right direction. They were alive—they'd been eating crawfish from the creek, sunflower roots, and any other kind of survival food they could think of, while they waited for somebody to find them. They'd kept the fire going with deadwood.

But it was crawfish Candy caught, sunflower roots

Candy dug, deadwood Candy collected. Rick had slipped and fallen into a gully Saturday afternoon, and shattered his left ankle. With Candy's help, he'd managed to get back to the tent. But that was as far as he could go.

Candy was fine. She was just tired and hungry and dirty.

"I told him how scared his wife was," Harry told me, "and he asked me if I could take him home even before I took him to the hospital. I wish you could have seen it, Deb. That's one divorce that sure as hell won't last."

"So now and then we do get a happy ending," I told Aline.

"Yeah, but it's damned rare," she answered, and looked down gloomily at the lists in her hand.

"There's not going to be any easy way to do this," I said. "Let's try this—I'll give a name and you see if it's on your list, and then you give a name and I'll see if it's on my list. That way we'll both get eyestrain at the same rate, anyhow."

"Let's get on it," Aline said. "I checked about half the first page of my list against yours while you were on the phone, so I'm a little ahead of you. Alton Sanders."

I checked my list. "Uh-uh. Dan Wentworth."

"Uh-uh. Crystal Boston."

I checked my list again. "Uh-uh. Judy Tyler."

"Uh-uh. Look, you better give names and let me look, because your list is about ten times the length of mine."

"Okay," I said. "Robin Carlyle."

"Uh-uh."

"Valentine Smith."

"Are you kidding?"

"That's what it says."

"A famous name in literature, but not on my list."

"Carl Gilbert," I read, and then I looked up.

"You know Carl Gilbert," Aline said, looking at my face.

"Not to know. But—he's Patrick's brother-in-law."

Aline looked back down on her list, running her finger carefully down the list of names. "Carl Gilbert," she said, and closed the list over her hand. "Not much use looking for other matches, is it?"

"No," I said, "not really. Susan said it would be somebody I'd recognize."

"Susan?"

"This friend of mine. She's a psychiatrist. I asked her to—sort of try to match the crime with a personality."

"You mean like the FBI does? Or says they do?"

"Like that. Only Susan's really a psychiatrist. Not an accountant with a month or two training in psychology."

"I think your Susan was right."

"I think I'd better call Castillo."

"What do you want to call him for?"

"Aline, he blew away a mail carrier. The feds have him on that. We have him on a kidnap-murder. But I'll bet the feds want him worse than we do."

"I'll bet they don't. But you're right. Castillo ought to be in on it."

I called Otto Castillo, halfway hoping, despite what I'd said to Aline, that I wouldn't be able to find him. But of course I did find him, and it took him exactly six minutes to get from his office in the federal building to my office in the police station. That is a distance of about ten blocks. Ten long, crowded, downtown blocks, with a parking garage at each end.

Unless he left his car in the middle of the street, and there are some streets you don't leave your car in the middle of if you want to find it there when you get back. I couldn't guess how he'd done it.

Otto had left his car in the middle of the street all the same, and when Aline and I pulled out he pulled directly in behind me. He was going to let me lead, because I knew the area a lot better than he did, but he didn't plan to get more than one car-length behind me.

Roma Gilbert was at home alone; the two children had been sent back to school, and her husband was at work again. "Mind if we sit here and ask you a few questions?" I asked.

"No, not at all." Whether or not Carl had anything to hide, Roma didn't. She looked no more than mildly puzzled at the entry of three different law enforcement officers from three different police agencies.

"What kind of work does your husband do?" I asked.

"He's an insurance salesman," Roma said. "He wasn't doing real good in Houston, and we decided finally to come back to Fort Worth because the cost of living is so much better we thought it would kind of balance out."

"Has it?"

"Well, kind of, I mean we're certainly not rich but we are doing better. Why are you asking about my husband? I thought you were trying to find out what happened to Patrick."

"We are," Otto said, "but we're trying to find out all we can about his friends. That should help us to figure out the whole thing. Patrick was pretty close to Carl, wasn't he?"

"Oh, yes," Roma said, "and I appreciated that, because the rest of the men in the family, seems like they all just dropped him. Richard never even came home for one visit after that awful thing happened, and Oliver wouldn't have much to do with him, and Billy Jack wouldn't, and Audrey's husband, he never came to Fort Worth much anyways but I never heard him say anything more than hi and bye to poor Patrick. Seemed like everybody had to take sides and everybody else took Sonny's. Well, of course Carl was sorry about Sonny, but he knew Patrick was too, and if the other men wouldn't have much to do with him, well, Patrick needed the friends a lot more. And really it wasn't Patrick's fault."

"Really?" I asked.

"Susie put him up to it, really. She did things like tell Patrick if he really loved her he'd fight for her, that kind of thing."

"I've never heard that before."

"Well, it's true," Roma said. "Carl told me so. She really was an awful woman. She did terrible things."

"That's not quite the way Lantana tells it, or Billy Jack," I said. "Wonder why they tell it so differently?"

She smiled. "Oh, Billy Jack was a little sweet on Susie himself. But of course Lantana didn't know that."

"But it was Carl who told you all this, not Patrick or Billy Jack, right?" I said loudly, and then wondered why I was talking so loudly. Did I really think I was going to penetrate through that head of hers?

"Well, yes, because Patrick didn't want to talk about it in front of me, but he didn't mind telling Carl, and of course Carl told me about it so I'd understand."

"When do you expect Carl home?" Otto asked.

"He usually gets home about five or so."

I looked at my watch. Three-thirty.

"If you like, I can call him and ask him to come on home," Roma offered.

"That won't be necessary," I said hastily, noticing the aghast expression on Otto's face. "We don't mind waiting."

"Well, let me get you a cup of coffee, anyway, then," Roma said.

Otto and I said "No thank you" almost in unison, but Aline said, "I would be just absolutely tickled to death to have a cup of coffee."

"You could come over here and join me at the table," Roma said. "Deb, you and your—your friend—don't mind sitting over there on the couch, do you? I could offer you some ice water, but that's really the only other thing—"

"We're fine," I said. The farther from coffee the better. It was really smelling awful to me these days.

And then Aline picked up a little silver bowl from the table. "This is pretty," she said. "Deb, come and look at this bowl Mrs. Gilbert's keeping M&M's in, would you?"

"Well—"

"Please come and look." Aline's tone was a little too dulcet, but Otto picked up on that seconds before I did.

"I think I'll have a look myself," Otto said. He strolled over to the table, and Aline held out for his inspection a small Paul Revere-style bowl of a brushed silvery metal. On one side of it was an outline map of the contiguous United States; on the map were the letters SA.

"That is nice," I agreed. "Where did you get it?"

"This place Carl used to work," Roma said. "It was a part-time job; he sold insurance most of the time, but as I said, he just wasn't quite making a living selling insurance, and he worked part-time at this other place, I forget the name of it, right after we got back to Fort Worth. He'd worked for them before in Houston."

"Was that an award for selling the most magazine subscriptions or something?" I asked.

"Oh, no, he got that for working there five years. But he did sometimes get awards for selling the most subscriptions in one night, and that sort of thing." She looked at me, puzzled. "How did you know it was selling magazine subscriptions?"

"I've seen the logo before," I said hastily. "What kinds of awards—"

And then Otto interrupted. "This isn't legally illegal but we're just about up to technically illegal. Mrs. Gilbert, I've got to tell you that we suspect your husband of being involved in several major crimes including kidnapping and murder, and you don't have to answer any questions we ask you. You have the right to remain silent—"

Roma Gilbert looked stunned. "I don't know what you're talking about," she said, her voice suddenly gone flat. "Carl wouldn't do anything like that. I don't believe Patrick did either. I think somebody framed him and murdered him and now you're trying to frame Carl—"

"Roma, we don't want to frame anybody," I said softly. "You've known me forty years; you ought to know I wouldn't frame anybody. We want to get the person who really did it. But we want that person bad. And if it does turn out to be Carl—"

"But it can't be Carl!" She started to cry, thinly, grabbing a Kleenex from a box and twisting it in her hands. "It can't be Carl. Carl and Patrick were friends, Carl wouldn't have killed Patrick, and he'd never in a million years have killed a child, he's a good man and we've got two children of our own and you should see how patient he is with them when they're sick, you're wrong, it can't be—"

"Then you don't mind if we ask questions," Aline said softly.

"You just ask all the questions you want to!"

"Your husband used to work at SellAmerica, right? Isn't that the name of the place you can't remember?"

"Yes, that's right, SellAmerica."

"Did they ever give him a red nylon windbreaker?"

"Why yes, I believe they did."

"Will you get it for us, please?"

"I certainly will. I told you, we don't have anything to hide." She headed for the far end of the house; in a moment we could hear her vigorously rummaging through the closet.

"She hasn't the slightest idea," I said. "That poor woman—"

"Yes, that poor woman," Otto said impatiently, "but then on the other hand you could look at Jared French, trying to raise seven children by himself."

She came back, head high, eyes defiant. "I can't find it. He's probably got it in the car, come to think of it, it was a little cool this morning."

"It was seventy-one degrees when I got up," Aline said.

"Well, it was cool here."

"All right, let's talk about something else," Otto said. "Does your husband own a green nineteen fifty-seven Chevrolet?"

"Well, he did, but he doesn't anymore."

"What did he do with it?"

"He loaned it to another collector who's probably going to buy it. I certainly hope so; I mean, I'm certainly not a woman who objects to her husband having hobbies, but he's spent so much time and money on it, and I'm sure when he sells it he'll get quite a lot out of it and we can certainly use the money right now. He gave me two hundred dollars last night and said that was just what the man paid him just for the option to buy it, and I must say I had a place for every penny of it."

"Oh? You're in debt then?" Otto asked.

"These days who isn't?"

"That's true," I agreed.

And then we all sat still. I wondered whether I ought to ask her where her husband was Saturday, where her husband was the day Helen French was kidnapped, wondering how far I could push my luck. I had my mouth open to ask when the front door opened and the substantial-looking man I'd last seen at the funeral service walked in with a briefcase in his hand, stopped short, and said, "Oh, hell."

"Carl!" Roma said, "your language! What are these people going to think?"

"Roma, tell me who these people are and what they're doing in my house?" But his eyes said he could make a reasonably good guess without being told.

Otto stood up and said, "Mr. Gilbert, I'm Otto Castillo. I'm a United States postal inspector, and I'm investigating the murder last Saturday of a mail carrier a few miles from here." He pulled out his identification as he spoke; I quietly unsnapped my holster, and I could see Aline, on the other side of Otto, doing the same. "I'd like to ask you a few questions, but before I do I must warn you—"

Roma wept quietly as Otto recited a Miranda warning.

"Do you understand these rights as I have explained them to you?"

"Does it matter?" The man put down the briefcase on the coffee table.

"Do you wish to give up the right to remain silent?"

"I don't think that matters much either, now, do you?"

"Not really," Otto said. "But it's still your right."

Carl Gilbert moved the ashtray to the side of the coffee table, so that he had room to open the briefcase. "Here's the money. Most of it. I used a little. I—we didn't mean anybody to die. I hope you can believe that." He looked at Roma. "I'm sorry, Roma. I really am. But that bitch Susie ruined the whole family and I figured she owed it to us. Nobody was supposed to get hurt. Jared French is all right. I sold him an insurance policy once. But I knew he had plenty of money, he wouldn't miss a little, and Susie—we were going to make sure Susie knew it was Patrick and then she wouldn't let him report it. But he wouldn't anyway. He told me—while we were talking about the insurance policy, we got to talking about crime, and he told me if one of his kids was ever kidnapped he'd pay anything before he'd let them get hurt. He said he wouldn't tell the cops because the cops would tell the papers. I didn't know the little girl would die. We didn't mean her to. There was plenty of air in there, Patrick even drilled a hole to make sure there was, and we picked a cool cloudy day so it wouldn't get too hot. We were just going to keep her in the trunk till we got out of Dallas and then get her out and put her in the back seat, and then I went to get her and she was dead. There wasn't any reason she should be dead."

"Did she cry, Gilbert? Could you hear her crying?" Otto asked brutally.

Roma Gilbert was crying.

The wrong people always are the ones who cry.

"We heard her cry for a little while. I yelled at her to stop crying and pretty soon we'd get her out and get her a soda pop. So she stopped crying. She wasn't supposed to die. Nobody was supposed to die."

"She had asthma. You knew that, didn't you?" I asked.

"Yeah. But I forgot."

Roma gave a little scream then. "Carl, how could you forget when you've got asthma yourself?"

If Susan had been there she would have been looking triumphant. But Susan wasn't there, and Carl Gilbert was talking compulsively.

"We were trying to figure out what to do with her and we were out driving in my car because we were going to change license plates and make it look like Patrick's car was my car and my car was Patrick's car, you know, and we were going to take her out and dig a trench with the tractor and put dirt over her and plant winter rye over her so that nobody would ever know, and we couldn't get the tractor going, and Patrick said we needed some part or other, and we went to get it and we couldn't get it in the back seat and the trunk lid jammed for some reason so we couldn't get it open so we put it in the front seat and Patrick was sitting in the back seat. And then the shotgun we had in the front seat—"

"Why'd you have a shotgun in the front seat?" Otto interrupted.

He shrugged. "So—in case we got stopped. That's all. I don't know why. It just looked like a good idea at the time, that's all. Anyhow the shotgun kept bouncing around the front seat slamming against that damn tractor part and Patrick said hand it to him and I started to hand it back to him and a stupid deer ran across the road and when I hit the brakes the gun—just—went off. That's all. It was an accident. Really it was."

"Was Bassinger an accident too?" I asked. "And Bill Livingston?"

"Livingston?"

"Livingston. The cop you hit on the head at the farm-house."

"Oh. Him. No, it was just—I had to get the money. I'd left it at the house. So I—I waited. Till I thought the cops had left and then I went in the back door and that's when I realized the cop was still there, just walk-ing around in the yard, so I—I waited till he came back up on the porch and sat down, and then I just hit him on the head a little. That's all. He didn't die, did he? I didn't mean him to."

"No," I said, "he didn't die. He'll recover, after a while. But how come you thought he was gone? Didn't you see his car?"

"Yes, but I didn't see him. So I thought maybe he'd just gone off and left the car and maybe somebody had given him a ride. Nothing ever works out right for me. Like Bassinger. I was damn sorry about that. I didn't want to kill him. I knew the old man. But he knew me too. And he saw—look—there was—stuff—you can't imagine—all over the back seat. I had to burn the car. Even Patrick would have agreed I had to burn the car. It wasn't my fault Bassinger came along—"

"No. It wasn't your fault," I said. "Nothing was ever your fault, was it? You knew Susie committed suicide?"

"Susie—did what?" He looked stunned.

"She killed herself, Gilbert," Aline said. "She killed herself. Susie Kelly—Susanna French—shot herself. Leaving seven children behind."

Roma screamed once. Just once, and then put her hand over her mouth to keep from screaming again, and then took her hand away from her mouth and said,

"Carl. That night. At the party. Before—before any of it happened. It was you who came in and told Patrick Sonny and Susie were in the grape arbor. I remember. Why did you do that, Carl? When you knew Patrick's temper? Why did you do that?"

And then I remembered . . . remembered that last thing I had blocked out of my mind, from that horrible Sunday school picnic when I was sixteen. I remembered Susie. I remembered Susie running toward them both, trying to stop it; I remembered that Susie was close enough when Patrick finally fired that Sonny's blood spattered over her, and I remember Susie stopping and screaming, standing with blood splattered all over her face and arms and hair and her pretty yellow summer dress, poor silly pretty Susie screaming, screaming, screaming, standing alone while my Sunday school teacher led me away and all the other women stared at Susie with accusing eyes—*it must have been your fault—it was your fault.*

Somebody must, finally, have taken care of Susie. But I couldn't remember who. And I couldn't remember when. I just remembered her screaming, for a very long time, with her eyes dry because she was too much in shock to cry, and I remembered the rest of it. The unforgiving eyes of the pastor telling Susie she was going straight to hell for this, while Susie went on screaming.

Gilbert shook his head and forgot to stop shaking it. "I didn't mean it. I didn't mean it. Nothing ever works out like I mean it to. Nothing ever did. Not ever. No. I didn't mean that to happen. Not any of it. Poor little Susie. Dead? Really dead? I didn't mean—she wasn't really bad. She was just kind of silly, that's all. She wasn't screwing Sonny. She never would've. She was just being silly. I—made up stuff. To tell Patrick. To talk him into stuff. Patrick didn't have no imagination. But I didn't mean anybody to get killed. Not Sonny, not that little girl, not Patrick, not Susie. It was just—to get the money—the money. And to get even with Susie— she'd talk to Sonny but she would never talk to me— and then later, living in that big ol' house, going to that big ol' church, thinking she was too good to associate with the rest of us mortals—"

Sometime while he was saying that I had crossed the room to Roma, and I had put my arms around Roma and she was crying quietly on my shoulder, but I couldn't stop thinking about Susie—Susie with blood on her hands—she must never have felt clean again.

Carl Gilbert was still talking. "Roma, I didn't want you to get mad at me for hanging around Patrick. So I told you stuff. It wasn't true. None of it was true. I made it up. I—just—was tired of being poor. Always being poor. All I wanted was some money. I didn't mean anybody to get hurt. I didn't mean anybody to get hurt."

I stopped, on the way home, by the Mossberg house. I'd never seen Rick. I wanted to see him, if he was home, if they hadn't kept him in the hospital overnight.

He hobbled to the door in a walking cast. "Who're you?" he asked.

"Just a friend of Deborah's," I said. "I thought I'd check in and see if everything's all right."

He gestured toward the couch, where Deborah Mossberg was asleep with a little girl cuddled beside her. "Yeah," he said, "everything's all right. Everything's fine."

"I'll come back and visit another time, when she's awake."

"You better visit when you've got the chance," he said. "Soon's this cast comes off my leg we're going to Germany."

"All of you?"

"All of us. Deborah says maybe it'd be fun to learn German cooking." He grinned. "I told her she better not get fat."

"I'll visit later," I repeated. "Just—tell her Deb Ralston dropped by."

"Deb Ralston. Okay. I'll remember."

We do get a few happy endings.

Even in my job.